SEDUCE ME

SEDUCE ME

A collection of twenty erotic stories

Edited by Miranda Forbes

Published by Accent Press Ltd – 2008
ISBN 9781906125929

Printed and bound in the UK

Cover Design by
Red Dot Design

Also Available from Xcite Books

The True Confessions of a
London Spank Daddy

Girl Fun 1

Slave To The Machine

The Education of Victoria

Naughty Spanking 3

Adventures of a London
Call Boy

Sex and Satisfaction 2

Ultimate Curves

Ultimate Decadence

Mistress of Torment

Naughty! The Xcite Guide to
Sexy Fun

Seriously Sexy Stocking Filler

For more information please visit
www.xcitebooks.com

Contents

Three's A Cloud
by Roger Frank Selby

'Come in Andy,' said Bill. 'Take a seat and don't look so worried!'

The Production Engineer of Swallow Fitness UK Limited, was lanky and quite handsome in the eyes of Olga but she pretended to study her clipboard as he folded into the armchair opposite her, facing the boss. 'I'll come straight to the point, sales are still crap and I have to let more people go.'

Andy jerked upright.

'But not you! I'd sooner close this factory down and start up again with just you, me and Olga. But keep that under your hat.'

Andy appeared to relax again, but gave Olga a dark look. Maybe he was jealous at her inclusion – after all, she'd only been here a couple of weeks. The boss was probably just being polite in her company.

'There's a chance of that then, Bill?'

'There is. More than a chance, it's a near certainty, unless we can come up with something really special. I've made the classic mistake of not diversifying my business enough.'

'But we make four completely different types of exercise bike.'

'Exactly, Andy. All exercise bikes! I should have branched out into other types of machine – or maybe equipment in a different market that uses similar production methods.

'Olga has come up with an, er, idea.' Bill began to look embarrassed. 'It's a pretty wild one, Andy, but it might just be our salvation ...' He glanced sideways at Olga and blushed deeply. She had an impulse to cuddle him like a little boy.

Andy seemed annoyed. 'With respect, Olga hasn't been here five minutes. She's just a temporary worker ... I mean she hasn't accumulated the in-house experience to know which way we should go, product-wise ...' He didn't look in her direction.

What a *scheisse!* but she let Bill do her talking for her.

'A naturally cautious reaction, Andy, but we must throw caution to the wind! We have to come up with something radical – and this could be it. Olga used to work in Hamburg. Something she once saw over there gave her this idea ... Hamburg can be a pretty wild town, you know ...' Bill's embarrassment at her idea began to exceed his enthusiasm. 'Anyway; Olga can show you ... Give you all the "ins and outs" – in the production office.'

Ins and outs? she thought – With Andy's hostile attitude? But she smiled for Bill's sake.

Here was Olga in his production office, with its shiny row of exercise bikes.

Sitting on the corner of his own desk, away from his respected boss, Andy adopted his normal cocky style. 'So what's with this Hamburg connection, Olga? Why was the boss so coy? Not about *sex*, is it?' Her enigmatic smile faded a little. He pressed on. 'Are we about to make sex equipment?'

'Maybe I should not be talking to you with your rudeness today.' But the smile remained. 'Perhaps I should take my idea elsewhere – I am only the *temporary* worker.'

Andy was in no mood to play games. Sure, she was a very attractive girl, with all the curves very much in all the right places, but she was really pushing her power. 'What did you do in Deutschland, Olga; did you work in the sex industry?' That wiped the smile off her face. She swung her arm to slap him. He stood and caught the arm easily; but only just blocked the groin-seeking knee-lift that followed.

Her attack brought him to his senses – he was harassing

2

this beautiful woman! 'OK, Olga I'm sorry; that was out of order.'

'Insulting bastard! Let *go* of me – this moment!'

'OK, but no more violence, promise? I *have* apologised.' He released her wrist and they separated, eyeing each other like a couple of sparring partners. 'Suppose you show me this great idea?'

'I can take you out, Mr Production Manager! I can take care of myself.'

'I believe you, Olga! You nearly took care of me just then … Look, we really have got off to a bad start. Call me Andy, please? And, for Christ's sake just show me this idea!'

She took a deep breath and his eyes couldn't help lifting to the rise of her breasts. They were pretty big without being too big. Probably a D-cup …

'My idea starts with a two-seater machine …'

'Is that it?' he interrupted. 'An exercise tandem? Olga, that's old hat; it's been tried before.' He sat down wearily and raised his arms in dismissal. 'They just don't sell.'

'*Nein!* That is not it, Mr Production Engineer!' She strode over to the office door and seemed about to make a slam-door exit.

She locked the door instead. Before he knew what was going on, she was pulling her blouse up over her head. Underneath was a semi-transparent white brassiere, pink nipples showing quite clearly through the material. She threw the blouse to one side, unhitched her skirt and let it drop to the floor.

Andy's jaw followed it.

'I'm just going to show you something. Do not be frightened; nothing will happen to you.'

She walked with long legs over to the bikes. Olga in motion was a gorgeous sight, her bra just controlling the jiggling of her well-formed breasts. She mounted the nearest bike and began pedalling. Andy watched fascinated.

The pedalling rhythm moved her entire body in a wonderful way. Tiny, high-cut panties nicely displayed the

3

rolling motion of her bottom, and linked by their brassiere cups, her lovely boobs bobbed around with a side-to-side oscillation.

'Now get behind me and imagine you were sat close behind, as on a tandem,' she ordered.

He jumped up and did just that.

'No, get closer. Imagine another set of handlebars just below my saddle, and that you're sitting on another saddle close behind. That's it; that's the first stage – what I call "Normal Tandem" You would pedal too, of course.

'For the second stage, those handle bars under my saddle are quickly removable. You have nothing to hold onto except me – so you hold my waist.' He held her slim waist while the orbs of her bottom rolled below – with panty material beginning to twist up into the valley between them. He felt his body becoming embarrassingly interested.

'Your hands go no higher, Andy – but imagine we were both without the clothes. What could you touch and hold from that position during second stage?'

She was way ahead of him. He mentally got a grip on himself. He so wanted to get a grip on her, those luscious tits wobbling around, just inches above his hands 'Every part of you Olga! And the *third* stage?'

'My saddle is removed completely, like this.' Her bottom lifted from the saddle and moved rearwards, swaying as she rode just above his lap. His discomfort was becoming painful as his growing cock tried to drill through his jeans to get between those mobile cheeks. 'Now there is nothing at all to stop the man behind from entering the bare, pedalling woman! So what do you think of *that,* Mr Production Engineer?'

'I have to admit it Bill, it's a killer idea. The tandem is not an obvious sex machine until you see a woman like Olga riding – then *wow*, you can see the concept straight away! The best approach to fabrication would be as an add-on kit … Bill?' Bill had a strange, hypnotised look.

'Sorry, Andy. I was just visualising Olga riding that bike. She must have looked … How far did she go?'

4

'She didn't strip right off, if that's what you mean, just down to her bra and panties. But that girl has one hell of a body! Talk about "X-rated!"'

'I know.'

'You do?'

'Well, ah, anyone can see that.' He thought for a moment. 'Do you think she would..?'

'Would what, Bill?'

'Well, er, strip right off?'

'Not for me, she wouldn't. There's not much love lost between us. It's World War Two all over again! But the fact that she did what she did, shows she might be up for it. But why should she?' he shrugged. 'What's the idea?'

'Well, we can't afford an expensive brochure for this bike. We'll have to use our regular printers and produce the artwork in-house.'

'Yes, but why …'

'I was thinking of using Olga in the brochure; she's a photogenic girl – er, I would imagine. She could model all the bikes in normal sports clothing …'

'… And then the tandem with *no* clothing?'

'Well, I can just imagine the Germans getting away with that, Andy – can't you? Maybe for once we could beat our competitors to the market with a new idea *and* a sexy brochure – if she agrees. Even just bra and panties might be enough.'

'I think they would, as it's Olga – but what a turn-on for the customers if she went that bit further – the same girl that they all saw dressed in her sports gear on the regular bikes, pedalling nude on the tandem! But will she do it, Bill?'

'I think she might if you asked her – after all, that's how she showed you her idea.'

'Not in the nude, unfortunately … I don't know … You're the boss; why don't you ask her?'

'I couldn't … You ask. I'm fairly certain she fancies you.'

'Really?'

'No!'

'But Olga, It was Bill's idea. I'm just the engineer,

5

remember? He gets a bit bashful around women – but he's a very good businessman; he came up from nothing ...'

'... And he goes back to nothing.' She looked a bit sad at that thought.

'He will do, if we don't help him through this. You came up with this clever idea; now we have to have a great looking model to sell the concept – you again! It won't be such a big deal; just start off modelling the regular bikes in your normal sportswear and see how it feels?'

She looked as if she was considering that.

'Then, if you feel like it, try a few shots in your underwear – just like when you showed me. You didn't seem too worried then.'

'I was angry – and no one was taking pictures! Who *is* taking the pictures?'

'I don't know. Our regular man, I guess – The one who did the last brochure.'

'But that brochure was so boring! I know a good photographer. He is the amateur, but he's excellent and I think he would do it if I ask.'

'But what would he charge?'

She smiled a secret smile. 'Oh, I don't think he'd charge us anything.'

'A boyfriend?'

'A friend.'

He shrugged his shoulders. 'OK ... great, Olga! You would do it then – if it's this photographer?'

'Well, like you say Andy, just as far as I feel like going, but this I promise you. The brochure will look so very good with this guy taking the photos ... and Andy?'

'Yes Olga?'

'I think *we* are friends now, Yes?'

God, she was beautiful when she smiled like that. 'Oh yes! I'm sorry I was such a prick to you before.'

'Prick?'

'Er, that's like, cock ... You know ...'

'But cock to me is nice, Andy.'

A few days later the tandem was ready, and so was Olga in her bright sports gear. Now there was a real back seat for him to sit on, Andy could hardly wait for Olga to be sitting there in front of him. They were back in the production office for an after-hours photo shoot, and their surprise photographer was converting the place into a studio.

'Hey, I didn't realise you meant the boss, when you mentioned your photographer friend,' Andy whispered, as Bill set up his backdrops and lights.

'I know, but I model for him before – swimwear at his photography club. That's how I meet him. He's OK with the women once he has the camera behind which to hide.'

'I had no idea he was into photography.'

'He is thought of very well at the club – one of those who use the real film on Glamour night!' Her giggle was infectious.

Hearing the laughter, Bill looked around nervously. Andy felt compelled to say something to include him in the mild joke. 'Olga was just saying that some of the guys in your club don't bother with film on Glamour night.'

He coloured a deep red. 'I never did see the point in that … Anyway, we're all digital now … OK, Olga, we'll do a few warm-up shots first of all, with you in that sportswear.'

'OK, Boss.'

She was pleased to be right. Once behind the camera Bill was a different man. He kept up a continuous stream of chat that relaxed her, and mirrored her own thoughts as he moved her around, posing her with all the machines. After ten minutes or so he probably had all the sports clothing shots they needed.

'Olga, if it feels right – and it *is* a bit warm in here – I'd like you to shed your top clothes – down to bra and panties if that's OK with you?'

'Yes Bill, that is fine by me. I'm OK. It feels good for me, with just you and Andy here.' It really did.

While Bill attended to his cameras and rearranged the lights, she slipped out of her sports clothes, aware of male glances, but feeling pleasantly cooler in the warm studio. She saw herself in the mirror. She looked good under the lights. The white underwear accentuated her creamy skin, but there was nothing understated about her shape, she thought, ruefully.

'Wow, Olga; you *are* the best!' Bill whistled softly, 'a real "hourglass" figure!'

Andy seemed really surprised at his boss; he'd probably never known him so relaxed with a woman before.

'You have seen it before Bill – at the club,' she reminded him.

'I know, but underwear is more intimate, somehow, and it will show in these pix.' He raised his camera. 'Now keep moving around Olga ... that's it, pose by it ... good. Other side now. Lean in ... get astride ... now right on the tandem. Ride it. Yes! Make love to it ... keep pedalling ... great!'

They worked liked that for several minutes, then stopped to rest.

'I wouldn't have thought bra and panties would look right on a girl on a bike, but ... they do on you!'

'But you really wanted some nude photos, right?'

'Well, how do you feel about that, then Olga?'

She knew exactly how she felt. She got off the bike, reached back and unhooked the bra in full view of the men. She shrugged out of the shoulder straps and uncovered her breasts. She knew the sight of her bare *titten* was having an effect on the men by the silly looks and open mouths. She let her breasts swing and jiggle as she laid the bra over a chair back. Then she gave the guys a side view as she bent over to push her panties down over her hips and thighs. She stepped out nude, stooped to tidy her clothing for a moment (giving them an eyeful of her bottom) then turned back to the men. 'Does that answer the question, Boss?'

The laughter relaxed everyone and the photo shoot continued like a dream. Bill would be getting all the shots they were ever likely to need of her on her own with the bike.

The shoot was going so well. Olga was happy, gorgeously

naked and relaxed. Andy was watching agog as she sported herself on the tandem, but Bill was secretly worried about how he would get the pictures he really needed – the ones spelling out exactly how the bike was to be used by a couple. Would Olga go that far?

'How do you feel about Andy coming into the frame now?'

She looked very bright – glowing with the exercise, and obviously enjoying her exhibitionism.

Her breasts rose and fell a little with excitement. 'Don't worry Bill. I know what pictures you need. I'd like to try that, but just the one step at a time … see how it feels, Yes?'

'You are a trouper, Olga! Now, Andy, keep your shirt and jeans on. You can be the guy who has just fitted the extra parts to make the bike a tandem. Now get on and just ride behind her, holding the handlebars …'

There was Andy, pedalling behind the naked girl in the viewfinder, emphasising her nudity and vulnerability. 'Oh, that's great! Fantastic!' Bill worked the shutter continuously.

'OK, Andy, while she keeps riding, slowly take off your set of handlebars. The intermediate shots will show how it's done… Yes. That's it. Now you have to hold on to her lovely waist. That's it Olga, work that bottom around!'

This is where we go beyond Glamour, he thought. He knew he was asking a lot of her – intimate contact with a man she hardly knew, while being photographed by another she knew only slightly better.

'Now, Olga, if you're ready, I'd like to take things a stage further – or we can take a break right now if you like?'

'No …' she breathed, 'I'd like to keep going.'

'Great. Now things get a little more overt. Olga, say "stop" at any time you don't feel completely comfortable with what I suggest …'

She smiled back at him, her full lips parted. He felt a rush of desire. Hey, what was going on here? She just fancied Andy, didn't she?

'OK then. Raise your hands, Andy; just touch the underside of Olga's breasts. Oooh that's it! Keep reacting like that, girl;

9

head back, shake those tits from side to side. Stroke them, Andy ... feel them a little more. Grab them. Raise your arms Olga, if you can, while he ... ahhh! Wow, Olga; they are lovely! Perfect. Don't touch them for a moment, Andy, while I get a few shots in ... lovely! Beautiful! OK Andy, caress them gently ... hey, don't squeeze them out of shape, let the camera see her nipples ... Yes. Lovely; keep them moving, keep everything moving ... That pedalling action sure works well...'

'Hey what about him – he still has all the clothes on!'

'Yes, Olga, that's the idea, it creates a power imbalance – although *you* hold the real power!' Bill couldn't get over the look of her naked. Without her knickers, her white thighs seemed to flow on up into her hips and waist – a continuous line up to her lifted breasts. And there was Andy, the lucky dog, touching and feeling her body – not as if it were his – but because she was letting a man do what had to be done to such a woman. 'We have a totally beautiful, totally nude woman riding on the front of our tandem; and a fully dressed man close behind. He is touching, caressing, feeling and squeezing her tits, her body – all over – as she rides ... and she is loving it, revelling ..., perhaps wanting ...'

'Yes – I want Andy in the front!'

'OK then.'

The couple swapped around. She pulled his shirt off over his head, and then reached forward.

As Bill zoomed in he could hardly believe what he saw through the viewfinder. Olga had unzipped Andy, and had him all the way out. He was pedalling madly, his legs akimbo.

'Shall I keep on taking pictures? Olga?'

'Yes ... It is OK ...'

'Ahh ... don't bother to ... ahh ... ask me then!' panted Andy

Bill smiled, but kept snapping away, watching her massaging Andy's shaft. These pictures could not go in any normal brochure, he thought.

She stopped pedalling herself and went round to Andy's far

10

side. She pulled off his jeans raising each leg as she did. He rode on naked as her mouth went down on him.

Bill took charge. 'Come round and do it from this side, Olga. I want to see your bottom as you bend over him.'

He moved in closer, photographing her breasts as they squashed rhythmically against Andy's thighs.

'Olga … when you're ready … Olga …'

She raised her head and looked at him with sleepy eyes. Her lips were wet and swollen with lust. Breasts swinging, her hand still held Andy's long cock. 'Yes, Bill?'

'Olga, I want you on the front of the bike again and Andy on the back – we have to show the final stage.'

Behind her again, Andy immediately had a clearance problem with her saddle. He removed it while she held her backside high. She began to pedal and her bare bottom rocked from side to side. Andy's straining cock seemed to be reaching right up to where it was designed to go, while her broad cheeks edged lower …

It seemed that the couple were going to couple anyway.

'That's it, Olga, let yourself sink back nice and slowly onto him …'

Olga did and Andy slipped smoothly up into her, all the way. She looked at Bill through half closed eyes as she groaned.

'Oooh, ahhh … Andy … start the pedalling!'

Andy pedalled slowly, the action sending him in and out of the woman at a measured pace. 'Now Bill, put down that camera and you come here now … put down the camera!' He did as she told him. 'Now you feel my *titten* as Andy pedals and fucks me.'

Bill took her big, pointed breasts in his hands, and felt their weight and movement as Andy rhythmically thrust up into her. She kissed Bill and opened her mouth to his tongue. He felt her hands working at his zipper and the wonderful release of his confined cock into her hands.

She transferred her wet lips down and took him all the way into her mouth while he tumbled and kneaded her breasts, and

11

Andy still pedalled on, thrusting into her.

Not a small man, Bill couldn't believe how much of him Olga could take in, but she did, somehow.

Inevitably, Andy started to come into her, but she kept working on Bill, with just a few muffled groans.

As he finished, Andy stopped pedalling and slipped out of Olga.

'Andy, off please. Now, hurry! Bill! You take Andy's place behind! Quick!'

'Eh, what? Me?'

'Yes, you Bill, now I want you inside me. *Schnell!*'

He kicked off his trousers and mounted the warm saddle just vacated by Andy; her broad bottom hovered invitingly above his lap. 'OK, Olga.'

She slid easily down, enveloping him like a tight, gloved hand. 'Ohhh! Now pedal, Bill, pedal!' Bill pedalled for all he was worth, and she began to howl out her orgasm, her inner muscles squeezing his slippery cock. Bill seemed to go on and on, thrusting into her, pedalling the virtual miles away. Maybe this was what she needed. Andy might be a bit younger and more spectacular but Bill had the staying power. She was still crying out when Bill finally climaxed, shooting his own wetness deep inside her.

Swallow Fitness' new brochure showing the company's nubile young board member, Olga Schulz posing nude on a tandem exercise bike with a clothed man behind her has caused quite a stir in the industry. CEO Bill Henderson, confirms that since the launch of the patented machine, and its controversial advertising, they have been swamped with orders.

Fitness Trade Magazine *understands that a number of competitors have looked into producing a similar machine to cash in on the boom, but the manufacturing patents, held by Ms Schultz appear watertight. For the time being, Swallow Fitness hold a lucrative monopoly in a new and intriguing sector of the fitness equipment market.*

Olga put down the article and glanced lovingly at the original bike that now had pride of place in her office, conveniently between her fellow directors' offices. It was nearly time for them to ride her.

She smiled wryly, wondering how that *Fitness Trade* journalist would report the extraordinary board meetings of Swallow Fitness UK Limited.

Yes, Tim
by Sommer Marsden

"Fu-uh-uck," I hissed. I dragged the word out while trying to back my SUV up without crashing into anything. Or killing anyone. "Please do not let me kill a worker," I sighed, inching backwards. I was completely blind. I did not want to end my day with manslaughter.

"Ho!" I slammed the break so hard I shot forward. The cans rattled and shifted in the back of my vehicle. The smell of old soda and beer made my stomach roll over. It was a cloying scent that would linger for days.

A face appeared at the door and I started. I pushed the button and the window whined. "Sorry. I can't see sh--crap. I didn't flatten anyone, did I?"

He gave me a small but friendly grin. "Nope. And you didn't dent your truck. That's the main thing. Pop the back for me?"

His face was long and lean. Weathered without being aged. Prematurely silvery hair that had once been blond it seemed. His eyes were the colour of steel and his lips were thin without being pinchy. Overall, a handsome face that made me feel calmer. I read his name tag. Tim.

"Sure. No problem."

I hit the button and heard the back door disengage. I opened the door and it thunked the concrete wall. I was a tad close. "Shit." Now I had dented it. I sucked in my breath and squeezed between the wall and the SUV. Once around back, I started to unload the huge bags of crushed cans into a pile.

My small company collected cans from the employees. We

kept all the cans from our modest business meetings. Held weekly, they were small but generated a surprising amount of recycling. One of my design clients went through a six pack of diet soda per meeting. I figured by the time I had finished her Zen-meets-punk-rock bathroom, she'd make up roughly a third of our can collection.

Every month I cashed in the cans and the proceeds went to a local charity. It was my small way of giving back to the community and doing something positive with the people who worked for me.

"– gonna get ruined." Tim was staring at me. What had he said?

"I … uh … what!?" I shouted. The place was possibly the noisiest place I had ever been and that included the circus and the rock quarry during blasting.

"I said, your shoes are gonna get ruined!" he yelled as a huge machine spilled a waterfall of aluminium into a giant bin below. Imagine if it rained rocks. And wrenches. With a few hammers for effect. I shoved my fingers in my ears and cringed. How could he hear at all? I'm surprised they weren't all deaf.

"It's fine! They're old!" I said and jumped when a huge boom filled the warehouse.

He laughed and guided me to the open bay. His hand on me made me feel warm. I looked again at his face. Nice face. Warm, friendly face. His hand was clean but busted up from working with metal all day. It looked out of place and completely right on my brown suede coat. "Your coat will get ruined in there, too. You've never been here, I take it?"

I shook my head. Somehow my gaze had become pinned to his lips. Pale pink. So pink they almost looked like he had lipstick on. Completely incongruous with his masculine appearance. I found myself shifting a little bit at the thought of those lips coming down on mine. On my lips. On my belly. On my hipbones. My thong rubbed over my now swollen clit at just the right moment and I sucked in a breath.

"It's OK. It's old," I breathed. And tried to tear my gaze

from his mouth. I managed to do it. My eyes fell upon his grey Dickies jacket and the wide chest underneath. Lean and tall, Tim was what I looked for in a man. No excess. Every muscle, every ounce put to good use.

"Still. Don't want to ruin something perfectly nice and useable. No waste. Remember?" he said and winked. His big hand slid up my forearm and rested at my elbow. He held my arm that way. Somehow completely proper and completely irreverent at the same time. Heat shot through my arm, up into my chest and flushed my cheeks what I could only assume was a cherry red.

"Right. I'm sorry. I didn't realize that they shouldn't be in so many bags. My assistant Tammy usually brings them." As I was explaining, a worker was ripping open all the little grocery sacks that held the cans.

"It's fine. Really. That's what we get paid to do. Right?" Another wink and a squeeze of my elbow.

I felt more than my cheeks flush and my breath caught in my throat.

"Listen to boss man," said a laughing voice. I turned to see a smiling Mexican man. He had a lilting accent and an easy grin. "That's what we get paid to do. You da man. You talk like one of us."

"I am one of you," Tim said. He smiled at his worker and then at me. It was clear this was good natured ribbing.

"Yeah, yeah. You wield the whip."

"Yes. I am a whip-wielder. I am brutal," Tim said. But when he said it, his face was a bit more serious and he squeezed my arm a little. I didn't take it as a threat. But I wasn't stupid. He held a strength and a serious nature that was thinly veiled behind that easy smile.

"I'm sure you are," I laughed. OK. I tittered because I was suddenly nervous. And I wanted him. I could kid myself and waste the time or I could admit it. I chose the latter. I very much wanted to have Tim fuck me senseless. Whip or no whip.

"Fucking rich bitches thinking we got nothing better to do,"

17

said the other man. It was clear by the look on Tim's face that this was not good-natured ribbing and not OK.

"Peter, you can go to my office. I'll finish up."

Rich bitch? I nearly laughed. I had scrimped and saved to become independent. Eaten more peanut butter sandwiches and Ramen noodles than I cared to remember. The smell of Shrimp noodles still made me gag. I flustered and clenched my fists. Then I covered my ears and yelped as Tim pulled a lever and another river of cans rained down from the sky.

When it was done, I did the only thing I could think to do. I was pissed and hurt and oddly attracted to him. So I worked. I opened bag after bag and handed them to Tim who dumped them in the sorter. On my final squat I felt a nice icy breeze and realized my white lace thong was not peeking, but popping up over my waistband. Probably half my ass was visible. I patted it with my hand as my throat seemed to close. Dear Christ. I had mooned him more times than I could count.

"I'm sorry. I was enjoying the view too much to speak up." And there was that grin again. Ready. Slow. Sensuous.

I wanted to smack him. I wanted to kiss him. Shove my hands in his grey-silver hair and see what those lips really felt like. I wanted to scream. Instead I said, "How much did it come to?"

His grey eyes probed and I hid my embarrassment. I had spent years polishing myself and here I was, smelly, sticky, with my ass hanging out. I had been called a fucking rich bitch, which was a riot. I was abnormally attracted to the owner and all I wanted was to go home and take a shower. And drink a bottle of vodka. Alright, a few drinks. Not a whole bottle. Hopefully.

"Let's see." He tapped the computer. Somewhere in the building a huge bash sounded. I read the sections. Copper, Iron, Lead, Aluminium. Anything to keep my eyes off of Tim. "Fifty two pounds. Name?" His eyes slipped over me, showing his interest.

"Jessie. Jessie McCarthy," I stammered.

He hit the print icon and the printer spat out an invoice.

18

"Sign this and ..." he stopped and smiled. The corners of his eyes crinkled in the most appealing way and I wished for the warmth and solidity of his hand on my arm again. "... and follow me, I guess because Lana is gone."

I looked at my watch. It was five already. After five, actually. "I'm sorry. You're closed."

"Spoiled," said Peter as he sauntered out. He looked pretty proud of himself. "I waited in your office but you never came. And now it's quitting time. So, I'm leaving. Unless you want to pay me overtime to rip me a new asshole."

Tim scowled. "I want you in on time and back in my office in the morning."

"Yep." Peter started to stomp off but Tim put a hand on his arm.

"You owe the lady an apology," he said.

I wanted to say he didn't. To tell him to never mind. The look on Tim's face told me not to. Hush, it said. Be quiet and let me do this.

"I'm sorry," Peter ground out.

I nodded.

But he kept talking. "I'm sorry that you're spoiled and rich and that you had to come in here and smell us and hear us and be around us working folk."

My father was a janitor. My mother picked crabs for a buck an hour to earn extra money. I had baby sat and delivered newspapers to add to the family income all through school. Spoiled was so far removed from me that it wasn't funny.

"You can clear out your locker, Peter," Tim growled.

Peter nodded, laughed and spat at my feet. "Gladly. Plenty of jobs out there for a low life like me." And then he was gone.

"I have to go."

He nodded and didn't argue. "Come on and get your money first. Don't forget that."

"Right. Sorry."

"No. I'm sorry. He's an asshole and I'm damn ashamed that someone like that could work for me. And you're not

19

spoiled. Anyone who's worked an honest day can tell that. He's just too hung up on what he doesn't have to see what's around him."

"How did you know?" I asked. "That I'm not rich. Never have been."

"Cause the rich women do not squat down and help slit open disgusting smelly bags of cans. Here you go. Twenty-five dollars and twenty cents." He handed me the money and his fingers brushed my palm. Lingered. Traced the lines of my hand. "Enjoy it."

"Not me,"

"Who then?" His eyebrow went up with the question and my stomach seemed to bottom out.

"Someone who might need it more," I said but then said no more.

I stopped for a latte. At the counter, I noticed the boy who was grinding the beans. His eyes, the colour of storm clouds. Not dead-on but close. His eyes made me think of Tim. I remembered how hot my skin felt when he looked me over the way he had. How they didn't seem to miss a thing. The feel of his gaze had been almost like being touched physically. I shuddered.

"You OK, Jessie?" Amy asked. She handed me my usual and I chugged a sip. It scalded like hell but I needed the fix.

"Nope. I am a spaz. I am sure of it. Now, will you do me a huge favour and make another one of these and toss some biscotti in a bag?" I handed her a twenty. "And keep the change."

"Oh, big spender," Amy said, working a liquid miracle with her petite hands. Within a minute I was holding another warm concoction.

"Yeah. Just call me Rockefeller, toots," I said and nearly ran to the car.

I expected to have to hunt for him, but he was the only one still at the recycling center. My heart stuttered when I looked at him. Serious face, big hands. I went wet between the legs when he gave me that slow grin.

"You're back."

"I am. Here." I handed him the coffee and shook my head. Very smooth.

"Thanks." Tim sniffed it and then laughed. "Vanilla?"

"Yeah. I shoulda realized it's kind of girly," I said. "Maybe just regular coffee. Or espresso." I shrugged.

"No. I like vanilla. I like coffee period."

Then he set the cup on the work station and touched me. With one finger. He slid his finger up my arm to my shoulder. He paused while I tried to breathe. Then he traced the line from my shoulder to my clavicle. My skin felt like it was on fire.

"I … uh …"

"Listen. You should have stuck around. About Peter," Tim leaned in and smelled me. Inhaled me like I was an elusive scent.

"Mmm?" I could feel his breath on my neck and my nipples went tight. Sensitive.

"He hates everybody. Even old Joe. A regular. Joe who has about five dollars in his bank account and one tooth. And it's not even a good tooth," he whispered and pressed his lips to the slope of my throat.

A bubble of laughter escaped me. My pussy was thumping now. A pulse that kept time with my briskly beating heart. God I wanted him in me. Some part of him. Tongue, finger, cock. All of the above. I couldn't remember wanting that bad. Needing. Seeing a man and thinking, *I have to have him*. I looked at Tim again and fisted my hands to keep from stroking him through this work pants.

"That's terrible."

"That he hates everyone?"

"No. That Joe's one tooth isn't even a good tooth."

"Ah," Tim said and slid his finger below the waistband of my jeans. His skin seemed to brand me. Heat and want flickered through me wickedly. My knees felt ready to sag. "Come on, girl," he said and took my coffee from me. I let

21

him. Then he snagged my two wrists in his one hand and led me. I went willingly. I would have gone anywhere he tugged me. We walked through the door marked OFFICE and he shut the door. The click sounded loud in the tangible silence.

"I don't normally do this," I blurted. I don't know why. I wanted to explain.

"I'm not in the habit, either," he said. Then he started popping the buttons of my white blouse without a word. "I want you out of all this."

His work scarred hands worked against the crisp white cotton. The buttons like little pearls in his big fingers. "Yes, Tim" I agreed.

I shucked the shirt like it was smothering me. His fingers worked over my plain white bra, gently pulled down a cup and released a nipple to the cool air. Then his tongue captured it and the warmth was shocking. "Fuck. You are gorgeous."

I grabbed his head with my hands but he snagged my wrists again and pinned my arms above my head. Against the shelf that held folders and boxes and ledgers. I liked the feel of being at his mercy. It made my cunt frantic. All I wanted was for him to fuck me. However he wanted. It didn't matter to me. Just the sensation of it was all I asked for. Just that. Nothing else.

His other hand tugged at my jeans. Wrangled my zipper. Pushed at them until they obeyed and slid down over my hips as I wriggled to help them along. His lips never left me. They nipped at my mouth, slid over my throat and my shoulders. Rolled hot circles around my exposed breast. I pushed into him. Seeking and finding heat and his hardness. I wanted to tug at his pants. Find what was waiting beneath the stiff utilitarian fabric, but he held me fast with his big hand.

"Turn around, Jessie," he said and I did. I spun in his loosened grasp like a ballerina in a music box.

His belt jingled merrily and I held my breath. Anticipating his freed flesh coming in contact with mine. He bent me over a clean cart. The sharp scent of new plastic filled my head along with the sharper underlying smell of the plant itself. He kept

22

my wrists pinned but now they were held behind my back. I teetered on the edge of the cart, my belly pressing so hard against it that I saw stars. Then his cock found my soaked slit and I forgot about the spots and lack of air and everything else. He slid into me with a satisfied grunt. The sound alone had me teetering on the edge of coming.

"Stay still, girl," he said and I went limp.

"Yes, Tim." Not docile by nature, it felt right anyway. I absorbed his motions, accepted the hard length of him. I didn't move back against him. I took him in.

Tighter and then tighter still. I felt my body gearing up for release. I wanted it and yet I wanted to keep it in the distance. In the future. So I could have him here this way longer. Or better yet, he could have me as he wanted me for just a bit more time.

"Fuck, you are so tight. So tight. And your ass …" he trailed off as the first ripples of orgasm shot through me. Halfway through, he pulled his cock from me and I cried out. "Just wait. Shh."

And he shoved into my ass. The pain was intense. It ate up my pleasure and then somehow enhanced it. I came long and hard. The pain flowing through me, dancing with the pleasure that threatened to overtake me. I let my head hang limp as he clutched at me. His fingers bit into my imprisoned wrists. His free hand yanked at my hips. When he smacked my ass hard enough to make me bite my tongue, a single tear slipped free of me. But he was fucking me so hard and the pain was so good. I came again on a sob.

Tim lost his rhythm. His body beat against mine in a frantic tattoo and he came. His teeth found my shoulder and nearly broke skin.

We stayed that way for a moment. Me teetering on the edge of the receptacle. Him buried deep in my ass. Softening but still hard enough to fill me.

"Did I hurt you?"

"Just enough," I laughed.

"Coffee's cold, I bet."

23

"Have a microwave?" I asked. His hands smoothed over my bottom. The spot where he'd struck me was hot and sensitive. He patted it hard enough to make me jump a bit.

"I do. Will you stay?"

"Of course."

"Better yet, come home with me?"

My body grew hotter. I didn't answer. I pulled free of him. My wrists sore and chafed. My ass sore and wet. My pussy ready for more of him. All of me ready for more of him. The way he was. The way he took from me. The way that made me feel. He studied my face. Steel gray eyes. Serious face. Easy smile. Then his lips compressed and he reached out. He grabbed my arms and gave me a squeeze. Hard enough to hurt.

"You're coming home with me."

"Yes, Tim," I said and smiled.

Mistress To Slave
by Morwenna Drake

Atia settled herself on the recliner so that the cool Italian breezes could play across her overheated skin. The bustling sound of the Forum drifted in through the windows and Atia breathed a sigh of contentment. She was glad to be away from the Northern Provinces and her father's olive groves. Life in the country was dull, with only a few servants to tend her needs while their villa in Rome afforded all luxuries a young woman could desire.

She heard Marcus's gruff voice announcing his arrival long before his heavy footfalls brought him into the room. Her feelings about Marcus were mixed – she knew of him as a magnificent businessman, his trading skills unrivalled, and he had always been decidedly attentive to her at each of their meetings. Her skin would tingle under his heavily-lidded gaze. Yet she couldn't help viewing him with a sense of despondency – as would any woman who met the man arranged to be her husband in a business deal.

Before he entered the room, Atia picked up a book of Juvenal's Satires and swiftly immersed herself in its pages, so that she appeared engrossed when he entered. Marcus strode over to the window without greeting; Atia matched his coolness and feigned concentration on her book, watching him out of the corner of her eye. After a few moments, he came to stand behind her, evidently looking over her shoulder.

'I'm not sure the barbed words of Juvenal are suitable for a young noblewoman's mind,' he said abruptly.

'I find his work quite stimulating,' Atia responded,

matching his gruffness with sweetness.

'Well, I shall have to see if I can't provide a more stimulating distraction for my future wife,' he said. Atia felt Marcus's hand on her shoulder and she nearly jumped at the unexpected contact, but she kept her attention firmly fixed on her book. He lightly brushed the nape of her neck, then her shoulder, moving down and slipping beneath the fabric of her robe. His hand cupped her breast, holding the globe in his palm while his thumb and forefinger teasingly tweaked her nipple.

Atia kept her gaze lowered, careful to keep her breathing regular and undisturbed, yet her pulse began to pick up speed. Marcus's caresses were slow and leisurely. Atia could feel the hairs on her arms standing up as her arousal spread through her belly and downwards. It had been a long time since she had felt the touch of a man, and she was taken aback by the strength of the desire which was building within her. Yet she knew she must keep her head – Marcus would be an unbearable husband if he knew he could control her so easily.

As Marcus's hand slipped across to her other breast, Atia realised she had read the same words on the page before her three times already. She knew her racing heartbeat must be giving away her excitement, and she tried to counter it.

'Really, Marcus, I find even the dullest of Juvenal's observations more arousing than that clumsiness you are attempting.' Atia cursed herself for the uncontrolled quiver which ran through her voice, undermining her impression of composure. Before Marcus could reply, a voice from the door made her jump.

'I have found them, master. They are in here.' Atia nearly dropped her book in shock to see her father's slave, Quintus, standing in the doorway. Marcus quickly withdrew his hand before Atia's father, Cornelius, appeared as well.

'Marcus, my apologies,' Cornelius said, his arms outstretched to embrace his future son-in-law. 'Quintus was most lax in informing me of your arrival.' As the two men embraced, Atia inwardly sighed; it was a favourite lie of her

26

father's to blame Quintus for his own tardiness. Cornelius was a man of bluffs – he gave the impression of an aging businessman, partial to snoozing over his scrolls in the late afternoon sun. Yet Atia knew that uncounted businessmen had been fooled into believing it to their cost.

'No apologies necessary,' replied Marcus with an indolent smile. 'I am sure a flogging will make sure he never does it again.'

'Are you suggesting I punish a slave on the first day of Saturnalia?' Cornelius asked with undisguised horror. 'Marcus, you know it is highly inauspicious at such a time for a master to berate his slaves. Why, it should be the other way round.'

Atia smiled quietly to herself, imagining any slave trying to berate Marcus. She doubted her future husband would allow such impudence, even during a festival where slaves where entitled to do just that. Marcus's sneer of disapproval confirmed her opinion.

'My family and I retire to our personal quarters during this unconventional time,' Marcus snorted. 'Of course, our most faithful slaves do not hold with such imbecilic frolics and remain to attend us. It is a frugal three days, but better that than having the house overrun by impudent slaves. Don't you agree, Cornelius?'

'Not at all!' blustered Atia's father. 'Why, even the most sombre of Roman citizens needs a little perversity in his life to keep him safe from the boredom bred by security.' As Marcus glanced aside in disapproval, Cornelius spared a wink for his daughter and Atia had to stifle a grin.

As the trio of men left the room to conduct their business, Atia was surprised to find Quintus's gaze resting on her for a moment. She returned his bold look with an innocent smile. Insofar as one could have any feeling regarding a slave, Atia had to admit that Quintus was her favourite. Dark and lean, with a bluntness to his brow. He was pleasing to look on – for a slave. He was never lazy or sullen and Atia knew she could trust his discretion about what he'd seen. Yet his departing look made her feel that he was nevertheless plotting something behind his subservient gaze.

The winter night had already closed in when Atia retired for her bath. In the country she was obliged to bathe in a simple, cramped tub, yet Cornelius's Roman villa had its own luxurious bathing suite with a large circular pool set into the floor. Atia leaned her back against the curved side and closed her eyes. She let the heated water cleanse her limbs and her spirit, trying to forget Marcus's earlier touch and the desire it had inflamed. Atia heard the door open and the sound of sloshing water as her personal slave, Arathusa, came to refresh the bathwater. Atia curled her toes in pleasure.

'I know you will be preparing for the slaves' feast, Arathusa,' she murmured sleepily, 'but would you rub some scented oil on my skin before you leave?' Any other time, Atia would have issued a command rather than a request, yet her father held strictly to the spirit of Saturnalia. He allowed his slaves to feast and game, attending only to the very basic needs of the family.

Atia held her arms out as Arathusa knelt behind her and poured oil over her neck and shoulders. Yet the moment she felt that rough touch Atia knew that it was not Arathusa who had refilled her bath and was now massaging her skin. She opened her eyes to see a man's hands wrapped around her forearms. She tensed and drew breath to protest but a familiar voice cut across her.

'Relax, mistress,' said Quintus, his voice deep but not as gruff as Marcus's. 'There is little point in my ministrations if you are too tense. Close your eyes and lay your head back on my lap.' The thought of protesting crossed her mind, yet his touch was firm, relaxing and his voice brooked no argument. Atia found herself doing as she was instructed without even thinking. As Quintus's hands moved to work on her shoulders, Atia briefly wondered what her father would say. Despite his strictness in keeping the spirit of Saturnalia, Atia suspected that a male slave helping his daughter to bathe might be a step too far. And the fact that Quintus had ordered her about in such a tone – even at Saturnalia – would undoubtedly infuriate him. The thought added a touch of delicious wickedness to the situation.

As she leaned into his massage, Atia could feel his dense calf muscles beneath her head, the rough fabric of his tunic brushing against her cheek. She thought how drastically different it was to the smooth silk of Marcus's fine togas. Quintus's movements were smooth and his fingers were agile, finding hidden knots of tension in her shoulders.

'I noticed you seemed a little … disconcerted when I came across you and Gaius Marcus earlier,' commented Quintus, the amusement in his voice evident. 'Were Marcus's attentions unpleasant to you?' Atia tried to remain calm and relaxed, although anger flared within her at his impertinent question

'I do not think that is any of your business,' she replied. Atia was painfully aware that it was almost impossible to carry off an indignant attitude when she was lying naked and oiled before him.

'My mistress's pleasure is one of my main concerns,' said Quintus in a low voice. As he spoke, his hands moved away from Atia's shoulders and slipped down to encircle her breasts. Atia drew in a sharp breath to protest, yet no words came. Just as Marcus's had done, Quintus's thumb and forefinger began to tweak and twist Atia's nipples. The oil on his hands heightened the sensation as Quintus squeezed the globes of both her breasts. Atia squirmed beneath his touch, sending ripples across the water to crash against the side of the bath.

'So this is to my mistress' pleasure, then?' asked Quintus. 'Or would she prefer it if I concentrated elsewhere..?' With his left hand still cupping her breast, Quintus's right hand began to slip downwards over Atia's chest and belly, and Atia raised her hips to meet his touch. Quintus's fingers curled for a moment in her most intimate hairs then descended lower to circle around her clitoris.

Atia gasped at his touch, moaning with pleasure as his

fingers found the entrance to her sex and slipped inside. Atia was positively writhing beneath his hands now, but Quintus suddenly withdrew his hands and sat back on his heels. Atia turned to glare at him in shock and frustration and Quintus gave her an apologetic smile.

'I hear the bell, mistress,' he said, getting up and adjusting his tunic, 'I must go and oversee the preparations.' The wicked smile he threw over his shoulder as he left told Atia that his departure was not as reluctant as he had intimated. Atia slapped the surface of the water in anger at being teased and unsatisfied for the second time that day. Yet the outburst did nothing for her frustration except to send bathwater pooling across the floor.

Cornelius and Atia dined together with preparations buzzing around them. Yet while her father wolfed down his dinner, Atia found herself without appetite, distracted by the sound of celebrations already underway in the street outside. A wave of relief soaked through Atia when her father finally dismissed her from the table. She intended to shut herself up in one of their receiving rooms in an effort to escape the raucous celebrations. As she went to retrieve a book from her father's study, Atia forced herself not to search out Quintus from among the household. At first she had convinced herself that she simply wanted to scold him for his earlier, inexcusable behaviour but she knew that if she probed her motivations deeper she would find her reasons for wanting to locate Quintus were quite different.

Passing through the atrium, Atia caught a glimpse of a pair of slaves in a darkened corner who had evidently begun their celebrations early. Her view of them was fleeting yet it was enough for her to take in the woman's head thrown back, her legs wrapped around the man's waist while his hips thrusted vigorously backwards and forwards.

The ecstatic moans of the woman followed Atia as she hurried across the atrium and through the archway into her father's study and closed the screen doors behind her.

Walking over to the balcony, Atia breathed deeply to regain her composure. She tried to subdue the jealousy that pooled within at the fact that even slaves were enjoying pleasures she had been denied twice today already.

With the cool night air washing over her fevered skin, she forced her breathing to slow and her heart to stop racing. In her mind she still saw the slave-girl, pressed up against the wall, only now the slave wore her own face and it was Quintus tangled between her legs.

'Lost in thought are we, Atia?' came a low voice behind her. Atia jumped, thinking she had been alone in the room. It was disconcerting to find the man who had dominated her thoughts all evening standing just behind her. He placed his hands on her waist to prevent her from turning round fully, and his touch seemed to burn through the thin, expensive fabric of her robe. It lit a fire in her skin which travelled through her belly and down into her loins.

'What happened to "mistress"?' Atia asked, trying to keep a disinterested tone. Quintus moved closer behind her.

'It's Saturnalia, when slave and master are equal,' Quintus whispered against her ear. His hands gathered up the fabric of her skirt and he had raised it to her knees before Atia pushed herself away from him.

'I am due to be married very soon,' she said indignantly. Quintus slid a hand behind her back and drew her close again. She could feel his swollen manhood pressing hard against her leg and her heart leapt at the feeling.

'Well? So am I,' he said with a grin before bending to plant light kisses along her neck and shoulder.

'You are?' asked Atia, genuinely surprised. Quintus slipped the sleeve of Atia's robe off her shoulder, following its fall with his kisses.

'A pretty little thing down in the Appian Way,' he murmured, his words muffled by her skin. Almost of its own will, Atia's hand snaked its way beneath Quintus's tunic and found the warm length of his shaft. Her heart hammered against her breast as she held it in her hand, so velvety and very firm. She kept her grip light and teasing, stroking from base to tip. Quintus had slipped both sleeves off her arms completely now, exposing her breasts to the cool evening air. He traced a decreasing circle with his tongue around one aureole to the hardening nipple at the centre. Then he took it within his lips, sucking on it until Atia's knees almost gave way beneath her. She had to lean on Quintus for support and this seemed to bring him back to his senses and his train of conversation.

'Yes,' he continued, his words punctuated by kisses, 'Melania has her master's permission to marry. She's a cheeky little thing – wild dark hair, and an arse so pert you just want to sink your teeth into it like a ripe apricot.'

'Like mine?' asked Atia idly, her eyes closing as Quintus moved his lips to encircle her other nipple. She started as he laughed.

'Good gods, no!' Quintus said. 'Your buttocks are anything but pert, Atia,' he said with a mischievous grin. Outraged at the blunt insult, Atia tore herself from his grasp and headed towards the door. Yet Quintus was too quick for her and, grabbing her from behind, he forced her forwards so that she was bent over Cornelius's writing desk. Atia squirmed in protest, but Quintus's grip was unyielding. She thought about crying for help, but an unexpected excitement growing deep within her made her bite her tongue.

'You misunderstand me,' said Quintus, raising the hem of Atia's skirt and exposing her buttocks to the night breeze. 'Melania's arse is firm and tight from all the work she does, but yours,' he gave a low, deep chuckle, 'your arse is soft and voluptuous, perfectly crafted by luxury and idleness. Your arse is designed for nothing but pleasure, dear Atia, and tonight,' Quintus paused to caress the smooth skin of her buttocks, 'tonight it is for my pleasure.'

Feeling his rough palms against her smooth skin sent a tingle of anticipation racing through Atia's body and she could feel her sex begin to moisten in arousal. She had invited men into her bed before, and some of them had been rough, but none of them had ever dominated her this way. Atia was uncertain whether, if she ordered Quintus to release her, he would obey. The thought that he wouldn't let her up until he had taken his pleasure from her sent a decidedly delicious shiver down her spine.

'I can see that, despite your indignation, you don't find my attentions entirely disagreeable,' murmured Quintus. Atia felt his fingers brush down her arse and begin to stroke at her exposed sex, coaxing out more of her juices until her intimate curls were slick and shining with them. Glancing over her shoulder, Atia could see an expression of intense concentration on Quintus's face.

'Push deep inside me,' Atia murmured, 'like you did earlier.' She felt Quintus's hand suddenly lie still against her skin and she turned to look at him in confusion. His eyes glinted with wicked delight.

'Why Atia,' he said in a tone of low reprimand, 'tonight of all nights you cannot order me to do anything. You may ask or beg, but any demands you make will be met with swift punishment.'

'Punishment?' asked Atia tremulously. 'What kind of – '

Before she could finish, Quintus raised his hand and brought it down behind her. Atia's buttocks exploded in a blaze of pain as Quintus administered a hard smack. She cried out in protest, but the blows continued unabated. Heat flared over her body, pain mixing with shame. Atia could only imagine what she looked like, bent over before him as he swatted her again, and again. The blows became harder and through the overwhelming outrage of it Atia found herself tipping her hips back, to take the slaps of his broad palm more fully across her buttocks. When Quintus finally stopped, Atia was breathless.

'This is intolerable,' Atia said, her whole body shaking with rage. She could hear the smile in Quintus's voice as he replied.

'No, my pet, this is Saturnalia. It is a time when social morals are turned on their heads, where a slave can be master

33

for a day. And for a long time, I have wanted to be your master, my sweet Atia.' Quintus bent low, tracing a path of kisses along the nape of her neck.

'Of course, if you'd rather I stop, all you have to is whisper, "please, please stop Quintus" and I shall leave you to your books without a word.' His voice was but a whisper now, his breath warm on Atia's skin where the evening air had chilled it. Yet the stinging pain in her arse had eased, to be replaced by a glowing warmth which spread down her legs and through her loins. Atia wriggled at the sensation, her pouting sex beginning to burn with desire.

'But I think you're enjoying yourself, Atia,' Quintus murmured, amusement rich in his voice. She shook her head in denial even as she felt herself grow slicker, warmer, more ready to be taken.

'Quintus, please …' she began, her voice a soft moan. She jumped when she felt his hands on her arse again, now moving in gentle and soothing caresses.

'Yes?' he asked expectantly.

'Please …' she repeated but her words were lost in a guttural exclamation of pleasure as Quintus's fingers stroked swiftly down her arse and buried themselves in her sex. He thrust them into her once, deeply, then withdrew.

'Turn over,' he commanded and Atia rolled on her back without question. She glanced down her body to see Quintus standing before her, his hand beneath his tunic stroking his erect penis. He looked at her with undisguised hunger. 'I'm glad to see you're getting better at obeying,' he murmured, his voice thick with lust. 'A little reward is in order.'

Quintus knelt down before her and buried his face in her groin, his tongue thrusting into her just as his fingers had done. Atia spasmed in ecstasy, thrusting her hips down so that his lips and chin were pressed against her. Quintus moved up to her clitoris, sucking on it and flicking it with his tongue.

Atia writhed with delight yet she felt as if there was an emptiness within her, with fulfilment lying just beyond the reach of Quintus's tongue. Bending forward, she pulled

Quintus's face away from her curls, and he looked at her with glazed, puzzled eyes. She pushed him to the floor, surprised at the strength with which desire had imbued her.

'What do you think you're doing?' asked Quintus, his own voice husky with desire. Atia felt she was near to bursting with frustration, unable to think clearly beyond the need to be satisfied.

'I need … more of you,' she stammered, her breath coming in short gasps. Quintus's eyes flashed with delight.

'Very well,' he said, 'but it's still my rules we're playing by.' In a flurry of movement, he had stood up, grabbed Atia by the waist and pinned her up against the wall. He hoisted her up bodily so that their eyes met. Atia was amazed at the strength in his arms and upper body which supported her. She wrapped her legs around his waist, pulling him closer until she could feel his penis pressed close against her sex. She began to lower her hips to sink down onto his shaft, but Quintus grabbed her buttocks and held her still. She looked in his face and saw that same wicked smile which had barely left his lips all night. She held her breath in anticipation.

'My rules,' he whispered, planting a tender kiss on the tip of her nose, 'and we'll begin when I'm ready.' Atia nodded helplessly, almost shaking with frustration. She had never been so completely at a man's whim before and it thrilled her.

Slowly, excruciating slowly, Quintus lowered Atia's hips so that she sank down onto his shaft. Completely supported by him, Atia wrapped him in her arms and buried her face in his neck. She couldn't help digging her nails into the skin of his back as Quintus withdrew then re-entered her with deliberate slowness.

The stone of the villa behind her was cold against her hot skin and Atia licked her lips as her breath came in short gasps. Quintus's thrusts were becoming faster, more vigorous and Atia realised she had no control over the moment. Her heart began to beat faster as she felt herself on the crest of an orgasm and she squeezed her legs tighter around Quintus's waist. She closed her eyes as the feeling intensified and

Quintus drove deeper and deeper into her. Her mind was filled with light, every muscle in her body tensed in anticipation. Atia cried out as the orgasm began to wash through her body, and she felt Quintus spasm within her as he matched her timing. She felt her fingers rake grooves in his back but she could not stop herself, she was completely lost in the moment. As she crested the peak of her orgasm, the room seemed to dance with light and colour. It slowly resolved back into darkness as her pleasure receded to leave her with a languorous inner glow.

Quintus eased her gently back down to the floor and smoothed away some stray strands of hair which had fallen over her face. Atia suddenly felt very self-conscious.

'We didn't even get undressed,' she said as she smoothed out the creases in her robe. Quintus reached out and tilted her head back to look into her eyes.

'Well then, that's a pleasure we can save for tomorrow night,' he said tenderly. He left her with a gentle kiss on her cheek, hastily adjusting his own clothes before disappearing out of the door. Atia picked up her abandoned book and, after a suitable delay, stepped outside the study herself. As she made her way to bed, her mind was already racing at the thought of the next night's adventures.

The Pleasure Fixer
by Candy Bagham

Abi loved her job. She remembered and relished every twist and turn of fate that had brought her to a career any twenty-three year old would die for.

To have some of the world's richest and most famous celebs relying on her, to ensure they could relax and unwind, was a very heady experience but, doubly gifted with charm and insight, it had only taken a couple of small triumphs to instil her with the confidence to take on the world.

She'd lived with Aunt Jessie since Mum had died, and Dad had fucked off to Australia with that slapper from the Royal Oak. Aunt Jessie was a gem; she endured constant pain from a gymnastics accident in her late teens but, despite it, took Abi everywhere she'd wanted to go. With her imagination perpetually stimulated by an endless appetite for the playgrounds of the rich, Abi knew she must have been a nightmare. Her butterfly mind had taken them to see to see fashion shows, weird art exhibitions, all the latest films and by the time Abi was fourteen Jessie had been to more gigs than the average rock journalist.

The part-time job at the hairdressers, run by Jessie's best mate Karen, had helped to pay for her obsessions, but they were still heavily subsidised by wonderful Aunt Jessie, and Abi was going to pay her back bigtime! In fact it was Karen who had added the final ingredient to Abi's encyclopaedic knowledge of all things celeb. Totally addicted to the gossip mags, she regurgitated every detail as she cut and coloured. No pop star could get engaged, or footballer get caught shagging his girlfriend's sister, without Karen knowing every tiny snippet. She knew how many times they'd been in rehab and whether they smoked or ate after sex.

At sixteen any idea of tertiary education was shot to pieces by the bizarre combination of 'A' grades in Maths and Art, along with 'Failed' in all other subjects. This recipe offered no obvious job opportunities, and she certainly wasn't going back to school for retakes. She'd hated it! The bores, the bullies, the fashion victims and the nerds – and teachers who symbolised failure with their lack of fervour or ambition, collectively they offered all the inspiration of a house brick. No! She wanted to go and meet the world head on, whether it be sink or swim, but instinctively she knew she was a strong swimmer.

Sure enough it wasn't long before opportunity tapped her on the shoulder. The job at the events company had been an amazing stroke of luck. By schmoozing one of the road crew, she'd managed to blag her way into the after-show party at the 'Crawling Ants' gig and ended up talking to one of the girls who did catering for bands. After a couple of JD & Cokes, and an offer of some 'E', Abi realised she was being chatted up. It gave her a real rush, like waiting on a ledge to do a bungee jump. 'Why not? she thought. 'Go with the flow, girl. Live a little!' The lights were wild and the pounding beat of non-stop music fired her up, so when Gina dragged her off into a corner, and pressed her mouth over Abi's, she found herself loved-up and responding willingly. Gina grabbed her hand, pulling her towards the door, she held back for a moment but as soon as she saw the look of eagerness on her new friend's face, she knew she'd be going.

The cabbie nearly drove off the road trying to watch them snogging passionately in his mirror, and the appreciative groan that had escaped her throat, as her seducer's wandering hands found a nipple, didn't help his concentration either! Gina directed him to a street in Tooting with terraced houses on one side and a railway line running along the other.

"Whada we owe you mister?"

"Thirty-one fifty, darlin'."

38

"What!" the girls chorused.

"After twelve innit!"

Gina rummaged in her bag for a moment "Sorry mate, seem to have come out without any money. Take an IOU?"

"Very funny. No dough then I'm calling the law. I've had enough rip-offs."

"No need to get nasty. How about we work it off?" she winked at Abi "How about a blowjob – from both of us. Bet you've never had that before. Here look at this."

She wrenched Abi's T-shirt up to her neck, cupping one breast and stroking it invitingly. A mixture of shock and excitement flew through Abi's mind and body. She leant into Gina smiling at the cabbie who had revolved in his seat.

"You serious?"

"It'll be the best night you've ever had in this old banger. Come back here, there's more room."

He scrambled into the rear and slid down into the seat as Gina pushed him back. Committed to her fate, Abi began undoing his belt as Gina slid down the zip and rummaged in his pants, coming up with quite a respectable erection.

"Ooh, what a big boy!" she crooned "Think he needs a bit more air around him, up with your bum!"

He raised himself, allowing her to slide trousers and pants past his knees.

She winked at Abi again, who was fiddling with shirt buttons, trying to avoid being captured in a clinch. "Think we ought to rubber him up, darling, don't you?" Abi nodded weakly. "Give us a hand then." Her hands dived into her bag and, as soon as Abi had leant away from the rampant cabbie, she produced her mobile.

"Smile please!"

She shot two quick snaps.

"Oy, what you doin'?"

"Think the law'd like to see these, you wanker? Come on." she said, grabbing Abi's hand once more.

They ran to a footbridge over the railway cracking up with laughter and stumbled to the other side.

"He'll never get round here before we're gone. Did you see the look on his face! What a toss-pot!"

Gina was a wonderful lover, and totally over the moon when she discovered she was initiating Abi into sapphic pleasures. She delighted in her ability to arouse. Greedy and giving at the same time, her fingers and tongue explored every centimetre of skin, every follicle and every orifice. She quickly extracted two mind-blowing orgasms from her apprentice. Now it was her turn! Clasping Abi to her breasts, she implored her to bite gently while she took two of Abi's fingers and inserted them deeply into her sopping cunt, writhing until she came with deep moans of intense pleasure. Abi kissed her passionately, her tongue probing, snaking round that of her lover. Then Gina held her face, looking deep into her eyes, before pushing her gently south.

"Now eat me. Taste what you've done. Use your fingers and your tongue, I want to come again."

The seductress slumped back on the bed, sensuously stretching her sinuous dusky limbs to the four corners. A little shiver of rebellion shot through Abi, inspiring her to take her time and savour this new experience. Taking charge, she slipped a pillow under Gina's bum, presenting her mons for the final sacrifice, then slithered to the foot of the bed. Nestling against a foot, her lips unhurriedly slid over the nearest big toe – a shudder of pleasure went through the other girl, and her fists balled as she grabbed two handfuls of sheet. Abi let her tongue find its way between each toe, running scratchy nails down the sole of her victims foot, while her other hand gently massaged up the calf, finally tickling softly behind the knee. At precisely the right moment she stopped, reaching out to take an ankle in each hand, she forced the long legs a little wider apart – just to state her dominance.

Her interest turned to the other foot where she began repeating the little tortures of ecstasy. Now she began to lick her way lazily upwards, from ankle to thigh, first outside then inside, until her face hovered close to Gina's pussy. It gaped a little because of being thrust aloft by the pillow and Abi could see droplets of come sparkling in the fine hairs around the lips – without touching it she returned to her task. The subtle team of tongue and nails trailed inexorably upwards, lingering on a flattened breast, eventually finding a dark nipple to tease. Groans of suppressed excitement escaped Gina's clenched teeth as the teasing flickers arrived in her armpit. A kiss brushed her lips, and her eyelids were licked softly, before Abi shifted her weight and began a downward journey on the other side. Gina whimpered, stretching out impatiently for her lover, only to find her arms pressed back into their submissive posture, pointing to the corners of the bed.

"Don't move." whispered Abi commandingly and, finding her discarded T-shirt, twisted it into a blindfold. Collecting the stranger's flimsy knickers which lay by the pillow, she wiped them between the lips of her still soaking cunt, then did the same to Gina before pushing them slowly into her mouth.

"You were very noisy before – we can't have you disturbing the neighbours now can we! You can enjoy our tastes while I enjoy yours."

Enough talk! She nibbled her way to the proffered breast, her nails stroking downwards until her fingers could mingle inquisitively among Gina's sparse pubes. Sucking hard on the pert rubbery nipple, she finished with a sharp little awakener before moving to kneel once more between her victims thighs. Here she revelled in the beauty spread-eagled in front of her, marvelling at everything that had happened that night. She relived her own orgasms, and remembered the way Gina's cunt had squeezed her fingers before soaking them, these memories heightened the awareness of what she was about to do as her mouth slowly approached her first pussy.

Resting on her elbows, a few inches from her target, she ran the tip of a finger down the lips, instantly feeling the heat. With both hands she gently peeled back the labia, savouring the rich scent escaping from within as she examined the pink entrance. Her thumbs slid upwards, pressing out as they went, until she could see the exposed tip of the shy clitoris, peeking out vulnerably from underneath its hood. Somehow she knew

41

exactly what to do! She sunk onto the nest of nerve endings and flicked rapidly – a muffled squeal of delight came from above.

Rejoicing in a wonderful sensation of power, Abi released the lips with her thumbs and ran her tongue up and down, parting them once more as the cunning muscle probed. She eased a finger gradually inside before drawing it back and rubbing gently around the oily ridges of Gina's g-spot, her insatiable tongue returned to rasp all over the rock hard clitoris. Approaching climax, Gina's hands flew to her sides, clenching and unclenching as she thrust up her hips to grind against Abi's mouth.

Abi stopped everything. "Put your arms back where they were." came the firm command.

A groan of frustration rose from behind the soaking knickers as Gina was denied the completion she craved – but she complied immediately. This reaction fuelled the sense of control growing so deliciously inside Abi, and she cruelly determined to take the desperately submissive girl right to the edge – at least twice more – before allowing her to spill over the top!

In the morning, no longer a virgin, Abi found herself gently stroking her still sleeping lover, taking in her willowy form and the perfection of her classically beautiful Indian features.

"Mmmn! How're you feeling?" murmured Gina, eyes still closed.

"Still excited at meeting my first lesbian."

Gina chuckled impishly "Sorry to disappoint, but I'm no lesbian. I like a bit of cock as much as the next girl – but you were irresistible!" She opened her eyes and kissed Abi gently.

"It's Sunday!" she announced with a grin "We've got all day to play."

"You taste and smell different from me, sort of musky, it's sensational!"

"That's cos I'm black. Didn't you know."

"No but I'm glad I do now!" laughed Abi "Anyway you're Indian. I wish I was like you."

42

"What, black?"

"No. Your body. It's fantastic! I'm fed up with being fat and there's nothing I can do about it."

"You're not fat, for God's sake, girl. Biggish yes, but you look amazing! Pretty face and wonderful big, firm tits and bum. Look at your waist for fuck's sake – no one could call you fat!"

Abi gave a wry laugh "They did at school, believe me!"

"School! Well fuck 'em ! Fuck 'em all! Look at you now! Who could resist you!" and with that she bent down and sucked a nipple hard into her mouth.

This time they took their time with their lovemaking and when Gina had got Abi's juices flowing liberally, she leant over to a drawer and produced a pink vibrator circled with white beads under a transparent latex covering and a little extension near the base. Gina moved down to lie between Abi's legs, making her pull her knees up for total exposure. She rubbed the head of the dildo against the folds of skin before easing it forward. It slipped in effortlessly, and the whole thing was soon buried to the hilt.

"You got one of these?"

"No." came the slightly shy reply.

"Oh good!" laughed Gina "Then you've got some nice surprises to come."

Abi heard the sound of an electric motor and suddenly the prick began to gyrate inside her. "Oooo!" was all she could offer. The tone changed and she became aware of the beads along the side of the shaft moving – Gina made sure they pressed firmly against her g-spot before carefully positioning the flexible tip of the rubbery extension against her prominent clit, and suddenly brought that to life too.

Each sensation on its own would have been enough to bring her to orgasm, but Gina's skilful variations meant that, as soon as one part of her pussy was ready to come, then she moved elsewhere. It went on and on and, just as Abi thought there was nothing more to come, she felt the moistened tip of her lover's finger scratching gently at the outside of her anus.

43

It built up lubrication as juices dripped from her cunt, and soon slipped further inside. At last Gina pushed the dildo home, the shaft writhed, the beads revolved and the vibrating tip lay perfectly against her clit. The most enormous orgasm explode throughout her body. She screwed her eyes tight shut, as flashes of colour went off inside her head and her ears rang with the blood pumping through her brain. She was conscious of the delicious sensation of Gina's finger worming its way steadily in and out of her arsehole as the seemingly endless intensity overwhelmed her.

The girls formed a deep and lasting friendship, they went out pubbing and clubbing, sometimes going home together, sometimes alone, and sometimes with a man. From time to time they'd spend a whole weekend at Gina's flat just chilling. Usually treating themselves to champagne or at least a decent wine. One of them would cook, they would massage each other, and the sex was amazing. An impressive collection of toys filled the drawer as their lively imaginations invented role-play games, occasionally with a bit of S&M. They'd tried it both ways, but by mutual consent it was Abi who tended to take the dominant role, she was more ingenious – and definitely slightly crueller. Twice now they'd shared a man, and Abi quickly realised how easy it was to manipulate the male ego into performing whatever she desired for herself or Gina.

As she had since her youth, Abi gravitated towards the celeb hotspots, now often taking Gina with her, and it was partially because of this that Alan, Gina's boss, had asked her along to help entertain a big talent agent, who might just offer Alan a run of gigs to cater. He knew the two hip girls looked good, and would be at home in a top club environment, so it was dinner at the new Quaglino's and on to Tramp.

'Biggy' Bardino was the American boss of the agency and he'd brought Peter Lipton, head of their London office, with him for the evening – a promising start for Alan! Abi found herself being monopolised by Biggy and, although he was obviously a shrewd hard-headed bastard, she couldn't help

44

liking him. He was fifty eight, overweight with receding grey hair, but witty and charming – in fact very good company. He enjoyed that ability which some Americans seem to possess of being direct to the point of rudeness, but somehow able to get you to reveal confidences.

"So whaddya wanna do girl? I mean really wanna do!"

Abi told him her dream. "I want to be a 'Fixer'. Specifically a Pleasure Fixer."

"You mean like a Hooker or a Madame? Hell that ain't so hard. Not much of an ambition though."

"Nothing like that. I've watched the rich and famous from all over the world totally unable to enjoy themselves. They're at the mercy of their fame – either the paparazzi, or some jerk demanding an autograph, hit on them wherever they go. Mostly they can't enjoy even the simplest pleasures without an army of bodyguards or a faceful of photoflash. I would be the Manager of their discretion."

"And what makes you think anyone would buy this? I don't think you understand quite how vain some of these guys are."

"Oh I know there's plenty who need the buzz of recognition. Despite their tantrums they'd collapse if they weren't in the news. But that would help me you see – 'cos they wouldn't be my clients."

"Ok, so Brad and Angelina want to go see The Stones – but they want to be in the crowd, not in the spotlight, and have an intimate meal out after. Over to you."

"Not too tough. Look-alikes, a little make-up and a little research."

"Ok Buffy – don't mind if I call you Buffy do you? Look just like her, a little bigger of course, but then that just makes you more beautiful."

Abi glowed at the compliment, even blushing a little, somehow it didn't seem corny because of the warmth in his voice.

"Ok Buffy, so give! How do you perform this miracle?"

"Well first they get tickets for the Royal Box, Restricted Area or whatever. Before the gig they go to a reception held in a private suite. Press are excluded. Then the switch happens. The look-alikes are hustled out into the waiting limo. Brad and Angelina are left behind getting a light make-up job, maybe a wash-out tint, glasses and a tash."

"And the same for Brad?"

"Very funny. Then they join a select little group of me and a few anonymous, definitely non-famous, friends and we all head for the gig like anyone else. My researchers will have told me what other celebs are at the gig, and we make sure the paparazzi know all about them, just to help keep them busy. Maybe even buy tickets for the latest B-listers who are causing a scandal. So – concert over, we grab a couple of minicabs and head off to the most fabulous little Italian restaurant I know, which hasn't been discovered yet by the rest of the world, and they get a table to themselves, a great candlelit dinner, a bottle of Chianti – and peace!"

The first job she got from Biggy was to fix up the latest James Bond with a tennis partner he couldn't thrash, and without a crowd of onlookers to spoil his game, this guy was a tennis obsessive! He gave her an unlimited budget, so when she found out that Rafa Nadal loved scuba diving and all water sports, and that Richard Branson's island was available, it was a cinch. She was cunningly choosy about the assignments she accepted, always being sure she could deliver, and not afraid to say no. Failure was not an option in this game.

Some months later, with her clientele growing and some big names using her number, Abi was sitting in her discreet little office above the hubbub of Oxford Street, making plans and contacts, when the phone rang.

"Hey, Buffy! Howya doin beautiful?"

"Good thanks, Biggy." replied Abi with genuine affection "How about you?"

"I'm great kid – but rushing as always. Listen, I've got Christian Warden in London, and I've told him all about you, he wants a meet to talk about some stuff. Can do?"

"Of course, my pleasure! He's about the hunkiest bunch of hormones on screen! Where is he?"

"Being chased down at the Ritz."

"Don't worry I'll fix him an apartment in Chelsea where they'll never find him. Give me a number."

Christian Warden – wow! She put the phone down and picked it up again straightaway.

"Gina, put your glad rags on. Have I got a treat for you! I'll pick you up at eight."

She eased the slightly milky silk stocking up her leg, and fastened it to a suspender clip dangling from the hand-made duck-egg blue corset, trimmed with a deep midnight lace. She never seemed to get a perfect fit from sixteen or eighteen so mentally called herself a size seventeen, but tailoring had to be the answer when she wanted to look her best. For instance these perfectly cut directoire knickers, fitting snugly across her lower abdomen, and scraping excitingly across the little triangle of bristle kept neatly trimmed at the top of her pussy, before slightly biting into the crease below. This time it was her own pleasure she'd fix!

With help from staff, she'd smuggled him out of the Ritz. He'd loved the apartment, he'd loved the champagne, he'd loved the Vietnamese take-away, and Gina had brought some great music and a little coke. And yes – he really was adorably charming and impossibly handsome!

"So Biggy says there's nothing you can't do – well I've got a bit of a list, maybe we could start to go through it?"

"Christian, I've never said this to a client before, but do you mind if we leave that 'til the morning."

"No problem. So what would you like to do tonight?"

Abi came up to him and placed one hand confidentially over his. "Well I need some really good sex – and so does Gina."

They stood up and began to strip. "Maybe we can put on a little private cabaret for you."

Twenty minutes later Gina was leant over the back of a chair, naked except for a thin gold slave chain round her waist. Abi stood in her glorious underwear, the belt from Christian's trousers dangling from her hand as the crack of her last stroke died away – she turned from Gina's rosily striped cheeks towards the bedroom.

"Follow me, slut!"

Gina rose and crossed the room submissively. As she went past Christian she reached down for the powerful erection he'd been stroking, and brought him with her. She whispered in his ear, slipping something into his hand.

Abi lay naked on the bed as the other two approached. Gina slithered down so they faced each other and kissed her friend tenderly.

"That hurt, you know."

"Good. It's what you wanted."

Gina's arms encircled her lover and smiled with anticipation as her leg hooked over Abi's and brought it forward – the movement exposed all of Abi's secrets.

Abi glimpsed the powerful figure of the unbelievably sexy film star lubricating his thick cock with the gel that Gina had passed to him.

"Mmmn. Thank you. I'll suck him hard again for you afterwards."

"I've told him you need it deep and strong."

"Mmmn," gurgled Abi again with a shiver.

"In the arse," added Gina tightening her grip so there was no escape.

Abi loved her job!

Shadow Play
by Jennie Treverton

Mirabelle and Adrian were having their first fuck in their new tent, when without warning Adrian pulled his cock out of her and said, 'Oh shit!'

Mirabelle yelped with shock. Adrian jumped up, grabbed the gas lantern and turned the light down as low as it would go.

'What on earth are you doing?' said Mirabelle, trembling with fury. 'That was so not the moment to bloody well ...'

She rubbed her clit, all hard and alive and abandoned.

'Darling, do you realise what we were doing just then?' he said, crouching down next to her. 'That light was giving everyone else on the campsite a detailed view of us having sex!'

'No, surely not.'

'Yes, I promise. What on earth was I thinking?'

He slapped his forehead.

'You're paranoid. Anyway, who cares? Look, here.'

She opened her legs and spread her lips apart.

'Can't you see what a state I'm in? Quick!'

'Of course, my darling, I'm sorry.'

In fact he could hardly see her in the gloom, but he could feel her arousal very well. He got his head down and stuck his tongue in her cunt, licking her to orgasm within seconds while pulling himself off.

When they'd got their breath back she turned to him and said, 'I don't think you could be right about the shadow thing. It wasn't the right angle for a start. And anyway, that doesn't

49

really happen except in stupid seventies films.'

'You don't believe me? Go and check for yourself. I'll set it up.'

He turned the light up full and placed it exactly where it had stood while they were screwing. Mirabelle pulled her dress on, unzipped the tent and went out. It was quite dark by now but the campsite was still busy. People were sitting at tables outside their tents and caravans, having dinner and drinking wine by lantern-light. If anyone had seen them, thought Mirabelle, she should be able to tell because they'd be staring, surely? But nobody seemed to look at her.

In truth, the thought that they might have been putting on a show for some unseen audience had made her even hotter in that moment. It had been quite an unexpected extra thrill. She was almost disappointed not to see anybody out here grinning dirtily at her.

'Mirabelle?' came Adrian's voice. 'How many fingers am I holding up?'

She walked away a few steps, turned and looked at the side of the tent.

There was an almost perfect outline of Adrian standing up, holding two fingers in the air. She could even see the short curls sticking out over his ears and the peaks in the line of his shoulders. The shadow was a little distorted, curving towards the bottom and getting wider and fuzzier until his feet disappeared, his legs like tree-trunks growing out of the ground. But everything from the knees up was razor sharp.

'Well?' he called. 'How many?'

'Um, is it four?'

'Four fingers? Are you sure?'

'Look, I really can't tell, you know. It's too blurry.'

'Oh,' said Adrian, sounding doubtful.

'It's just a sort of shadowy mess. You can hardly even tell it's a person.'

Mirabelle smiled to herself.

'Oh, right,' he said. 'Well, I stand corrected.'

*   *   *

The next day Mirabelle went to the beach to sunbathe while Adrian did some 'maintenance work', as he called it, checking seams, twanging guide-ropes, filling water-bottles. He'd been wanting to go on a camping holiday ever since they'd first got together more than three years ago, but each summer Mirabelle's choice had won. This year he'd summoned his courage, and in an obviously rehearsed speech he'd told her that he was sick to death of airports, and she'd love camping if only she'd give it a go, and she'd love Cornwall and she'd love the beaches especially.

Actually, it turned out he was right. This beach was small enough to be intimate, nestled in a curve of high cliff. It was only five minutes' walk from the campsite and she anticipated spending lots of time here, in this sheltered spot behind a fallen crag, if the sun stayed as warm as it was now. She lay back on her lilo, wearing her new purple and blue bikini and big sunglasses. She felt the breeze lapping at her edges and the sun heating her skin. She began to feel lazy and full, like a summer fruit hanging on a vine, and she stretched her arms out, putting her hands behind her head. Her fingers raked through her thick dark hair and rested on the nape of her neck. She spread apart and wiggled her sandy toes.

A shadow passed across her. She opened her eyes and saw Adrian, looking pissed off.

'Oh, hello,' she said.

'You're not going to believe this. We've just been landed with the neighbours from hell.'

Adrian had chosen a pitch among the trees towards the edge of the field, a little away from the tangle of tents in the middle, so that they'd have a bit of extra space around them. However, there was now another tent a couple of metres to the side of theirs. It looked quite old and shabby with strips of gaffer-tape on it and speckly patches of mould. The inhabitants weren't around but there were some carrier bags lying on the ground and some plastic six-pack rings.

'Look,' said Adrian contemptuously. 'They haven't been

here five minutes and they've already started littering.'

'Who are they then? Have you seen them?'

'Yeah, they came in driving a knackered old Astra. There's about six of them. Boys, boy-racers, whatever you want to call them. Chavs, basically.'

'You're such a snob, Adrian.'

'Don't have a go at me, I'm just telling the truth, that's all. You'll know what I mean when you see them. They're so bloody loud. They're going to make this holiday a sodding nightmare.'

'Oh dear. Well, maybe they won't be too bad. We'll just have to see.'

Adrian started picking up the bags and plastic rings, huffing and tutting.

'It's not your mess, Adrian, leave it.'

'That's not the point, it's the general state of things, isn't it. Oh, I don't know.'

He stood up and wiped his forehead.

'I'd like to have a word with Mr Kenwald and find out what he thinks he's doing, putting a load of hooligans next to us. Can't he find a more isolated place for them?'

Mirabelle thought that Adrian had probably chosen the most isolated spot already. She expected Mr Kenwald was thinking of the other campers. But she thought she'd better not say that to Adrian.

In the distance there was an aggressive farting sound. It grew louder and louder and then an old white Vauxhall Astra appeared.

'Oh, hurrah,' said Adrian.

The car trundled across and parked under the trees. They piled out, in high spirits, carrying more plastic bags filled with bottles and beer cans. The eldest boy must have been about twenty, Mirabelle thought, and the youngest about sixteen or seventeen. Most of them were rather unhealthy-looking with pale skin and spotty jowls. They had a sort of uniform, consisting of American football shirts, checked baseball caps, and gold chains. They had a sort of language too, a gabble of filth: it was all *fucking bollocks* and *fucking shite* and *what the fucking cunt?* Mirabelle wasn't sure whether to be frightened of them or not. They were all guffawing at each other's jokes and monkeying about the place, but she thought that somehow they didn't look such bad boys. One in particular caught her eye, one of the younger ones, who had wavy reddish-brown hair and freckles. He was a slender boy with long legs, narrow hips and a long back, and high, square shoulders like Adrian's. He had such a cute face with a pink Cupid's bow mouth. But he was so close to manhood, he reeked of it. He was so ready. And there was a knowingness in his eyes too, an eagerness. She couldn't take her eyes off him.

Mirabelle was quite shocked by her thoughts. Perving at boys more than ten years younger than herself!

They'd noticed her now. They were glancing naughtily at her and laughing at each other's hand gestures. She couldn't quite decipher what the fists and fingers meant. They were obviously in-jokes of some kind.

She wondered how many of them were still virgins.

Adrian said, 'If they give you any trouble I'll geld the little fuckers.'

While Mirabelle had been on the beach Adrian had made sandwiches for lunch, so they sat outside at their folding table to eat. He said that they should just try to ignore the boys as much as possible. But there wasn't much else round there to watch, so he and Mirabelle ended up doing a running commentary on the boys' antics.

'If they don't eat some solid food soon they're going to be sick as hell,' said Adrian.

'It'd be much better if they used the camp toilets instead of going behind that tree all the time,' said Mirabelle. 'It's going to stink of wee round here before long.'

Adrian snorted.

'They're doing a lot worse than weeing, mark my words.'

'What do you mean?'

'Come on Mirabelle. Boys that age? They've got no control over themselves. All they think about is getting the poison out.'

'You mean they're masturbating?'

'They're teenage boys. Of course they're masturbating. There'll be semen all over the place back there, believe me.'

Spunk like tree-sap. Mirabelle's eyes grew wide.

In the afternoon she and Adrian went down to the beach. As they sunbathed side by side, she found she kept daydreaming about the boys. She wondered what they were thinking about, when they were behind the tree, to get themselves off. They were so young, she could hardly imagine they'd had time to develop really corrupt fantasies. Would a nice pair of tits be enough for them? But there was so much porn available on the internet and suchlike these days that she supposed it was quite possible for a young boy to become a seasoned, jaded pervert before he'd so much as sniffed an actual woman's crotch.

That one boy in particular. If he was still a virgin, it was almost a crime. He looked as though he knew exactly what he'd do, given the chance. He'd done his research, he'd know where her clit would be, how to touch it, how to build pressure and friction. Perhaps he'd come quickly but his cock would be stiff again almost straight away. And he'd drink in every moment, every moan she gave, so he could learn everything about her response. God, what a treat that would be.

Later on, back at the tent, she rolled on to her side to face Adrian and said, 'Actually, they remind me of myself at that age. Me and the girls. Did I ever tell you we went on holiday together to celebrate finishing our GCSEs?'

'The Gower, wasn't it?' said Adrian.

He was sitting on the edge of the airbed, sorting the cutlery back into the roll-up case. Outside, the boys were playing dance music. They kept fiddling with the volume, so it would be almost silent, then suddenly flare up intrusively, then die back again. Occasionally they'd stop it mid-track and put something else on. It was difficult to ignore.

'That's right, Three Cliffs Bay,' she said when it was quiet enough. 'Beth's granny let us have her static caravan.'

'Were you a bunch of annoying bastard hooligans, then?'

'We were supposed to be there a week but we got thrown off after four days.'

'Really? I don't remember that bit. What did you get up to, you naughty girls?'

An explosion of laddish laughter came from outside. One of them shouted, 'Not again Boycey, you fucking minger!'

'The usual,' she said. 'Drinking, smoking, singing. Having boys back.'

'Boys, what boys? Did you fuck anyone?'

'No. Some of the others did.'

'So what did you do, then?'

He came and lay down next to her. His face was very close to hers and he began to pull at her dress straps.

'C'mon, spill,' he said into her hair.

'There was a boy called Simon, from Chester,' she said.

'And how far did you go with Simon?'

Adrian eased the front of her dress lower. He put his hand inside and began stroking one breast, then the other.

'This far?'

'Well, mm, yes,' said Mirabelle, and she stretched herself out so her nipples came out of the top of her dress.

'What about this?' he said and bent over her. He began lapping slowly at a nipple.

'Mm. Yes, but, mm, not quite like that. More sort of – well – more urgent.'

His tongue pressed harder.

'Oh yes,' said Mirabelle. 'Just like that.'

She arched her back, feeling her cunt give the first squeeze of excitement. She wanted more.

'The other thing he did, was – he got me to touch his cock.'

'No!' said Adrian between licks.

'And he fingered me.'

Adrian gasped.

A dirty thought occurred to her. She looked round for the gas lantern. It was turned up bright but it was hanging near the tent door. Totally the wrong position.

Then the music shot up again and the bass shook the ground, making everything buzz. His head came away from her tits.

'Oh for fuck's sake!'

'So I got my hand,' she said quickly, almost having to shout. 'Like this.'

She stroked the front of his jeans. There was some blood in his dick but it wasn't fully hard, like she'd expected it to be.

'And he did this.'

She took his hand and pushed it up under her hem and between her legs, where the juice had seeped through her knickers. But the hand was lifeless, completely forgotten by him.

'It's fucking intolerable! I don't see why we're putting up with this.'

Mirabelle sat up and sighed heavily.

'So what are you going to do, confront them? You say a word, they'll just be ten times worse.'

'I'm going to talk to Kenwald. Right now.'

'No, you're not. I need you!' she said, hearing the desperation in her voice and hating it.

'I'm sorry, darling. I can't concentrate. It's no use.'

He unzipped the tent and walked out. Mirabelle was outraged. She scrambled after him, pulling her straps back up.

'Adrian, get back here!'

'I'll just be a minute,' he called, disappearing into the dark.

'Bastard! If he thinks I'm following,' she said, and suddenly she became aware that it was very quiet. The music had stopped.

The boys were sitting round their fire, all staring at her. Wide-eyed, curious boys.

The rage inside her was unbearable. She saw the skinny boy on his feet not far from the tree. He looked like the rest of them, part defiant, part uncertain.

She had to do something.

She ducked back inside the tent, grabbing the gas lantern.

'So, you want to wank?' she said, putting it on the ground

and throwing her dress off. She faced the side of the tent.

'I'll give you boys something to think about.'

She took her knickers down, sticking her arse out, and turned to the side so they could see her profile and her high tits. She massaged her boobs, one in each hand, and then she bent her head and stuck her tongue right out, circling a nipple. It felt so good and she moaned, quite unable to believe how outrageous she was being. Then she switched sides, turning round so they could see her licking herself.

She heard a nervous giggle, some urgent whispering, then more silence. She could picture them, dumbstruck, their shorts straining at the front, hands straying down.

Now she touched herself between her legs. She was wet all down her inner thighs. Her clit stuck right out of her lips, hungry and so big. She fingered herself, still holding one tit up to her tongue with her other hand, and she wondered how she could show them what she was doing to her cunt. She held her hand clear from her body and just used one straight finger to tease the very tip of her clit. She moved her hips against the fingertip and threw her head back, luxuriating, moaning out loud.

'Oh my fucking God,' said one of them quietly.

'She's going to come.'

'D'you think she …'

'I'm going to fucking well come.'

'Oh my God!'

She was sure they were all tossing off round the campfire by now, she could hear the strain in their voices. But which voice belonged to that particular boy? In that moment, she thought they were all him, all the voices, and if she couldn't give him his first fuck, well then, she'd give him the next best thing.

Her finger was dipping into her slit quicker and quicker and she thought that she'd never felt so turned on in her life. Her legs felt weak but she had to stay on her feet. She needed something inside her now and she scanned the tent, looking for something with visual impact.

The first thing that came to hand was Adrian's camping torch. It had a grooved black rubber handle and when she gripped it she found her fingers and thumb didn't quite meet. She hoped it wouldn't be too thick.

She also hoped Adrian wasn't on his way back yet.

She turned to face them again, standing with her legs apart, and she held the torch as if she were a porn star, stroking it theatrically, admiring its dimensions. Then she pushed the end into her cunt.

'Oh Christ,' she breathed. It was really big. But not too big, just right in fact, and with a few movements it went in further and further.

Outside one of them groaned loudly.

She stuck it up herself, working her clit with her other hand. It filled her so deliciously that she knew she'd be coming very soon. She gyrated, turning this way and that, pushing her arse out so they could see it going in from behind. She teetered and nearly lost her balance as she worked the handle in and out. She couldn't keep standing much longer. Rubbing her clit frantically, she shoved the handle up and came, throwing back her head, freezing for an ecstatic moment, and then collapsing on the airbed with the handle still jammed inside her.

She wasn't sure how much time had passed when she felt Adrian sit down on the bed. She became aware that she was under the covers by now. There was a sublime ache between her legs. He was taking various items off the bed and putting them away.

'Darling,' he whispered, 'you must be careful not to leave clothes near the gas lantern. Your dress could easily have caught.'

'Sorry,' she said, rubbing her eyes, dazed.

'I don't think we'll be having any more trouble with that lot, anyway,' he said, taking his T-shirt off and getting under the covers. 'I just had Mr Kenwald down here.'

'Oh, did he talk to them?'

58

'Yes, well sort of. They were quite well-behaved in front of him, annoyingly. Either they're frightened of getting chucked off the site, or they've just knackered themselves out. They're pretty subdued though, turned the music off, the lot. Kids today, eh, no stamina.'

He kissed her neck.

'So Kenwald probably thinks I'm over-reacting. He had a word, anyway. Told them not to leave their filth all over the place.'

'Well done,' said Mirabelle.

She turned over, closed her eyes.

'They couldn't even look me in the eye, any of them. Scared shitless.'

'They're good boys really,' she murmured. 'Well done, darling.'

60

To Fly An Eagle
by J. Manx

The Eagles of 133 squadron transferred to Biggin Hill, Kent,
England, in May 1942.

133 was the first American squadron to be stationed there.

'Do you recognise any of it, Grandma?'

She was a sweet thing, my granddaughter. Twenty-five
years old and she reminded me so much of myself, full of life
and eagerness.

I was a little disappointed but not majorly so, I didn't really
expect it to look the same. Still, I had hoped there would be
similarities. But the orchards had gone, replaced by dull,
suburban housing.

'I can't say I really recognise it, sweetheart, so many
houses.'

My granddaughter looked disappointed. She'd planned this
as part of a birthday surprise, a return visit to the house of my
youth.

'Come on, let's go to Biggin Hill, I'm sure you'll
remember something there.'

I shuffled back into the car.

'Never mind,' I said, 'it's been a lovely day and I've really
enjoyed your company.'

We drove along the busy 'A' road and the housing became
less dense and the land became more open and the trees more
abundant. And then, familiarity. The shape of the road, the lay
of the land. I recognised several houses.

'I know that house,' I said, excitedly, 'I remember this

61

road.'

'See grandma, it was worth it.'

I remembered. The breeze in my hair, the laughter, the sun, the summer freshness and him. How could I ever forget him?

It was June 1942. I was nineteen.

'Can I see you again?'

I hesitated, not knowing how to react. I'd never been asked out by a man before.

It was the end of a thrilling evening. A dance. The first I'd ever been to and it was the first time since the war started that I'd had such heady fun. There were a lot of men from the Biggin Hill air base, but he stood out. He breezed into the village hall with two others, laughing and loud, and every girl noticed them. They stood in the middle of the floor as if they owned the place and he looked around and his eyes fell on me and my girlfriends and a big, bright smile spread across his face. He nudged his friends and walked over to us.

'Could you teach us how to dance?' he said. And he was handsome. He had friendly, Clarke Gable eyes and an Errol Flynn chin. He had Hollywood style. Of course I said yes. Coyness, playing hard to get, had its place but not if you might never see them again. He turned my head and left it spinning. He danced with me all evening.

Johnny Genarro. 'What kind of name's that?' I'd asked.

'My father's Italian, my mother's Irish, a passionate mix, could only produce a passionate son.'

Everything about him reflected his love of life and he just carried me along.

The orchard, that's where he took me that first time. Mum was a bit unsure, had circumstances been more normal I don't think she would have let me go. But this was wartime and Dad was away fighting and I think she thought why the hell not? And she could tell Johnny was OK, he won her over with his warmth. 'We're just going for a drive, Mrs Carter, won't be long; I promise we'll be back within the hour.' And he was, although it seemed like five minutes. He picked me up in a car he'd borrowed from his base. There were hardly any cars around in those days, we had the road to ourselves. And he took me to the orchard and it was there that I tasted my first kiss. I can still taste his tongue, the shock and the pleasure, and his mouth on my neck and the thrills coursing through me. Those first few times he took me back home spot on time and left me longing to feel him again. After a couple of weeks he got bolder.

'Is it alright if I take Janey for a picnic tomorrow, Mrs Carter?'

Mum was a little reluctant but she agreed. So he picked me up, gave Mum some tinned meat and he took me for a picnic and taught me how to fly.

He'd spread out the blanket and we sat down and then he took me in his arms. We kissed and I felt his shoulders and back and rough chin and the smell of his oiled hair and his masculinity, there was no deodorant in those days. I pressed my body into his, feeling its warmth and strength and his hands were on my hips and waist and bit by bit moved over my bottom, caressing then gripping. Without realising, I'd opened my legs and his hips were between them and I could feel his hardness and I wanted him but I knew I shouldn't and I had to push him away.

'What's the matter, babe?

'We shouldn't, I want to but we shouldn't.'

'I'm sorry babe, I just got carried away, you're so gorgeous. Here,' he said, leaning back and spreading his legs, 'look what you're doing to me.' He nodded down to his crotch. I could see a large bulge in his trousers.

'Is it uncomfortable?'

He undid his trousers and released his cock. It stood proud and rigid in front of me.

'Not any more it's not,' he said, smiling, a glint in his eye. I'd never seen a cock before. I was surprised by its size, it looked regal.

'Do you like it babe?' I was fascinated. 'Why don't you

touch it? it won't bite.' He laughed. I reached out and touched the tip. It twitched. I withdrew my hand, giggling.

'Do you know what a joystick is, Janey?'

I shook my head.

'When we fly planes we use a joystick to direct the plane. You move it around to control the direction of the plane. Now, if you learn to manage a man's joystick you can take him anywhere you want. Would you like me to teach you?'

He was still smiling that wicked smile and I laughed and nodded.

'OK, babe. First of all take a firm grip. Go on.'

I curled my fingers around his cock and was surprised by its warmth.

'That's it, babe, just a little higher.'

I adjusted my grip and felt the ridge of his glans under my curled forefinger. 'That's it, babe, perfect, now I'm ready to fly.'

I could feel his cock pulsing in my grip.

'Now, babe, with a plane's joystick you move it from side to side and back and forth, but with a man's joystick you move it up and down. Just give it a try.'

I moved my hand clumsily up and down his cock.

'Oh, babe, that's wonderful …now, a little bit faster.' He lay back and I watched his eyes shut and his hips push upwards as I moved my hand up and down his hard, warm cock.

'A little faster, babe, that's it …oh, babe …that's it.'

And then he bucked and ejaculated a spray of white semen and he cried out and I screamed in surprise. No one had ever told me about this. He laughed and I fell back giggling. He sat up.

'Oh, Janey, that was fantastic.' He cupped my chin in his hand and kissed me.

Johnny gave me a lot of flying lessons after that. It was such fun. I learnt the basics first, grip, tempo, pressure and having mastered these I moved on to other areas. And somehow my mouth was drawn to his cock. Delicious.

Smooth, warm and so beautifully hard and I loved the way it deflated after I'd drawn its precious juices. Then I'd stroke it back to its full magisterial poise and we'd start all over again.

And then the time he brought me to orgasm. I was on my knees, my head bent over his lap, one hand cupping his balls, the other gripping his cock. He'd been running his hand under my dress, up and down my thigh, brushing over my bottom. I was becoming agitated, I knew I shouldn't let him go there but my pussy was juicy and aching to be touched and I raised my bottom slightly and his fingers had eased themselves inside me. I sat on his hand and his fingers wriggled and played me to orgasm and all I could do was hold on to his cock and cry out into the summer air. After that, there was no stopping me. He christened me 'Plane Jane', and I got to fly him regularly, and his flying lessons became the focus of my life.

I used to see the planes flying over in formation and coming back from missions regularly, but I don't think I fully understood the danger they were in and the crucial role they were playing in protecting the country from invasion. It was only years later that I read about the Eagles, the Americans who volunteered to fight as pilots in the R.A.F., before their country had entered the war.

I turned to my granddaughter. 'I met my first boyfriend here,' I said, 'he was an American pilot, very handsome.'

She giggled. 'I can just imagine you holding hands together under an apple tree, must have been very risqué in those days.'

'Yes, I suppose it was.' I smiled to myself. Yes, everything was very innocent then, just as sex should be, but God was it exciting and exhilarating. I've never topped the excitement of those first experiences. My mind took me back to that last picnic. It was the beginning of July, another wonderfully sunny day. The day Johnny Genarro flew me to heaven.

We lay kissing and, feeling him harden, I pushed away from him and began to undo his trousers.

'Time to fly,' I said, easing his cock from his trousers.

65

'Final lesson today, Janey. If you pass this you'll get your wings. I'm taking you further than you've been, so you need to trust me. Do you trust me Janey?' His eyes had the devil in them, but a gentle devil. His cock, as usual, was rigid and I began to stroke and caress it. I hadn't seen him for almost a week and I was already wet, I wanted his fingers inside me.

I nodded. 'Of course I trust you,' and I parted my legs and he eased his fingers into me. Immediately, I began to gasp and Johnny watched me, smiling, then, just as I felt myself about to come, he withdrew his hand, rolled away from me and reached into his jacket pocket.

'Oh, don't stop, not yet, Johnny.' I was still gripping his cock.

'See this Janey?' He was tearing open a packet and from it he took out something I hadn't seen before.

'It's a rubber, it means I can really make love to you and we can both enjoy it and there won't be any risk.'

I watched as he sat up and rolled the sheath over his cock and I laughed at the sight of it and he laughed. Then he kissed me, rolled me onto my back, lifted my skirt and filled me and the sensation was indescribable and as he filled me, again and again, I kept shouting his name and then he withdrew. He knelt up and began removing his clothes and I did the same and then we lay naked in the fresh orchard and fucked and fucked and it was glorious.

Afterwards, as I lay in his arms, he reached over to his jacket and took off a small metal brooch.

'Here,' he said, laughing, 'you earned your wings today, Janey, you flew me to heaven. I don't think there's another pilot that could do that.'

I pinned the brooch to my dress.

'Well, it's a fine plane,' I said, 'you need a good machine if you're going to fly properly.'

He laughed and then he said, quite seriously, 'Janey, when this is finished, will you come home to America with me? You'd love it there and I can introduce you as the British flying ace that could fly a man to heights he'd never been and make him perform like no other. Whaddya think?'

That day was the happiest of my life.

I never saw Johnny again. He was shot down whilst escorting a convoy of bombers over Calais.

I fingered the brooch on my dress.

'He taught me how to fly,' I muttered.

My granddaughter squeezed my hand.

'I'm sure he did grandma, I'm sure he did.'

Fire Down Below
by Landon Dixon

You see plenty of wildlife from a hundred-foot-high fire tower. Especially with a pair of high-powered binoculars.

I was manning Tower #2 in the national park one fine, sunny morning, sweeping the treetops with my glasses for any hot spots, when I flashed on to some wild life that soon turned yours truly into one raging inferno. Two camping girls engaged in an early morning skinny dip.

Nothing too unusual, I thought initially. But as a Park Ranger fully trained in water safety, and legally constituted to enforce the ordinance on public nudity, I felt it my duty to monitor the situation; make sure the two women didn't get into any trouble, or cause too much. So I zoomed in on the bobbing water nymphs, pulling them right up into my cloud-scraping platform with the powerful lenses.

They were up to their necks in the sparkling blue wet stuff, but I could tell they were buff by their bare shoulders – not a swimsuit strap or bikini string in sight. One girl was a blonde, the other a brunette. They both had pretty faces, the blonde, blue eyes and a diamond stud in her right nostril, the brunette, brown eyes and the plushest pair of lips I'd ever ogled from distance.

They were laughing and yelling and splashing water at one another, enjoying nature in the raw; as I enjoyed their raw, playful natures. And telepathically urged them to move into shallower waters – where my hungry eyes could feed more fully.

But then something even more dramatic happened,

something that will be burned into my memory for ever, like the first time I met Smokey the Bear. The brunette dipped her head down and dove underwater. And then the blonde suddenly burst up out of the water and into the air, propelled skyward by her mischievous playmate, breaking the surface bare and glistening and big, big busted!

My eyeballs almost popped the glass lenses. Blondie's tremendous sun-burnished, tan-lined breasts flung up into the clear, blue heavens like twin Free Willys, water streaming off their velvety skins, pink nipples snouting up and out, poking holes in the sunshine. Until gravity did its worst and they and she flopped back down into the water with a heavy splash, swallowed up by the lucky lake once again.

I took a step back, tingling all over, a tree growing up in my Ranger-issue khaki shorts. Then I gave my dizzied head a shake and screwed the spyglasses back into my eye sockets. And was hit between the peepers by another thunderous set of breasts – the brunette's this time. She'd discovered the sandbar in the middle of the lake and climbed aboard, baring herself to the watching world from the waist up, showing off a pair every bit as breathtakingly large as her blonde gal-pal's, only tanned all over.

My legs buckled. My mouth and eyes watered, wooden pole tenting my shorts like the horniest of happy campers.

This was a fire tower once-in-a-lifetime observation too good to pass up without the proper acknowledgement. So, violating every rule of decorum in the Park Service book, I unzipped and pulled my log out into the open, commenced rubbing like a Jack London character desperate to build a fire.

Just in time, too. Because now Blondie had joined her breast-bud on the sandbar, both girls bare-chestedly exposed to the warm sunshine and my perverted, prying eyes. They danced around kicking water at each other, giggling and shrieking, boobs flopping and flapping, nipples bouncing.

My binoculars bounced right along, capturing the latticework of tiny blue veins all around the blonde's shockingly pink areolas, the satiny-white, untanned skin that was normally hidden by a swimsuit almost blinding me. I swung over to encompass and count the pebbles on the brunette's enormous, caramel-coloured nipple halos, to survey the entire gleaming, golden expanses of her breasts. All the while stroking and stroking and stroking my hardwood.

The binoculars shook in my right hand, as my cock stretched in my left. And then we hit Code Red on the Fire Warning Chart. As Blondie splashed over to the brunette and fell into her arms. And the two women stopped playing around and started fooling around.

They gazed into each other's eyes, their bodies and boobs pressed hotly together. Their slickened heads moved forward, arms squeezing tighter, until their wettened lips touched, stuck.

I had to wring the head of my cock like the neck of a chicken, to keep from exploding. Even Old Faithful would've blown early exposed to the blistering sight of those two freshwater mermaids lip and tit-locked together in a lovers' embrace.

I ogled the scorching scenery for all I was worth, not giving a damn if the whole picturesque, Congress-protected park went up in flames on my watch. And when Blondie caressed the side of her girlfriend's blossomed-out breast, stroking and rubbing the shining skin, I just couldn't hold back any longer. I had a raging fire down below and only one way to douse it.

"Come-bombs away!" I yowled at the smooching sirens, cock going off in my jerking hand.

White-hot semen jetted out of my cap and sailed clear over the metal railing, splashing down a hundred feet in the forest below, the whole tower shaking right along with me. I struggled to keep the jumping binoculars trained on the bussing, bumper-to-bumper babes, as I fisted like crazy, saluting their beauty and boldness with blast after blast.

Until, finally, they broke laughingly apart, just as the last of my seed soiled the earth down under. Holding hands, they plunged back into the deep water, submerging themselves and their, and my, lust in the warm liquid again.

71

I sank to my knees, totally devoid of warm liquid.

It took me a full minute to recover. Then I zipped up and then down, riding the tower ladder steel railings to the ground like I was sliding down a hundred-foot fire pole. Abandoning my post was the grossest dereliction of duty, especially with Big Betty, the arse-busting supervisor, due for inspection at any time. But this was a personal emergency of the highest urgency.

I piled into the Park jeep and burned pine needle, speeding out to the secluded beach where the hootered hotties freely frolicked offshore. And in five minutes flat-out, I was tumbling out of the rolling vehicle and racing over the grassy dunes that led to the water's edge.

Skidding to a stop at the shoreline, I was just in time to get another sizzling eyeful, up-close and in-person this time.

The girls were swimming around in the glittering water, and floating around. Plump, boisterous buns flashing edible enough to sink your teeth into when they paddled; ripe, round breasts and rubbery nipples bobbing luscious enough to wrap your hands and mouth around when they floated. I watched the erotic water ballet, cock pumping up again, kernels in my nut sack popping.

And just before the girls caught on to my presence, I managed to gather up my senses enough to gather up their clothing strewn all over the beach and toss the whole bundle behind a bush. Then I pulled out my whistle and blew taps on their skinny dipping.

"OK, ladies, out of the water!" I bellowed. Then held my breath.

They stared at me and my uniform. Then started swimming, splashing, crawling towards me, using the water to blanket their bodies.

"This is a family camping area," I croaked, when they were a mere twenty feet away from where I stood on shaky ground.

"Sorry," the blonde said sweetly. "We were just having a little fun."

72

The brunette nodded, grinning. "Yeah, we just got kind of carried away, I guess." She glanced over at her girlfriend, and they both giggled. "Could you throw us our clothes, please?"

I looked around – elaborately – but just couldn't seem to find their duds anywhere.

"Drat, someone must've stolen them," the blonde lamented. "You didn't happen to see any perverts lurking around here, did you, sir?"

Not without a mirror I didn't. Then added out loud, "I'll drive you ladies back to your campsite, and you can get dressed there." I didn't bother offering them any of the blankets we keep in the jeep.

They looked at each other, at the pressure-bulge in my khakis that was impossible to hide. And then they rose up out of the water.

I gazed at the dripping wet goddesses like the Greeks must've gazed at the Venus de Milo unveiled. Their breasts bumped and swayed, jounced and shimmied, as they waded towards me. And they were as bare below-the-waist as above; the both of them sporting strip-shaved pussies winking with moisture. My boggled eyes bounced back and forth between the pair like I was refereeing a game of nude beach volleyball.

"I'm Stacey," the blonde said, four feet, and thirty-eight chest inches, away from me; naked as my lust. "And this is my friend, Holly."

"P-park R-ranger P-phil," I stammered.

Holly lifted up her arms and arched her slightly chunky body, stretching, pushing her breasts out into the neighbouring state almost. "Mmmm, that sun feels sooo good," she purred. "And the water, too. We just couldn't help ourselves, Park Ranger Phil."

Stacey nodded, hugging herself around her ample waist and sighing, rocking from side-to-side. Her forearms all but disappeared, boobs swinging like overripe fruit on the vine. "You're not going to arrest us, are you, Park Ranger Phil?"

I didn't, couldn't respond for a moment, hypnotized by the pendulum motion of her breasts. "Huh? Uh no, no," I snapped back to life. "Usually I just issue a warning, or a small fine."

"Oh," Stacey cooed.

"That's fair," Holly breathed.

Sweat trickled down my palms and forehead, my cock throbbing in time to my racing pulse. As we all stood there looking at one another under the glaring sun.

Until Stacey suddenly strolled right up to me and touched the insignia on my left shoulder, her right breast reaching out and touching my bare arm, all warm and soft, rigid nipple pressing into corded forearm. "Could you possibly just let us go with a warning, Phil?" she asked.

Holly hit me up from the other side, running a finger along my hat brim, rack rising like buoys on a wave to swamp my right arm. "We'll be good girls from now on, Phil. We promise."

They crowded in on me, sandwiching me in sweet, splayed sensuality. I couldn't spit out a single word, my Ranger training useless in this unanticipated, but highly fantasized, situation. The wicked heat and flower-petal smoothness of the girls' boobs against my skin made my face burn and blood boil, like I'd taken a skinny dip of my own – in the hot springs. I was caught between the naughty, busty bathers, with no possible thought of escape.

And then Holly kissed me on the right cheek, Stacey on the left, their pressing breasts kissing the breath right out of me.

"You like our boobs, don't you, Phil?" Stacey whispered into my burning red ear.

"I-I love them!" I blurted, ablaze.

Holly laughed, wobbling her breasts and me. Then hissed, "Show us!", and grabbed my hat and flung it away, grabbed my bare head and pulled it down onto her chest.

She buried my fiery face between her pillowy boobs and I went limp as a noodle, held up only by her tits pressed against my cheeks. I could muster only enough strength to lick – straight ahead at the girl's breastbone, side-to-side at her tit-walls.

Then I was suddenly out. And gasping for breath. Then

back in again, between Stacey's breasts this time. She buried me almost to the neckline in her hot, damp, velvety cleavage, and I tongued her like I had Holly, my lungs burning, cock stretching the fibre of my shorts to the tearing point.

Then Stacey popped me out in a gush of saliva and pent-up air. And Holly slapped my face with her thunder-tits – one cheek, the other cheek – batting my empty head to and fro. Then Stacey, the girls working their boobs like padded love paddles, playfully pinballing my noggin back and forth. I never wanted the game to end.

Until Holly shoved one of her honey-dipped nipples into my open, drooling mouth, and I latched on with my lips like a hungry child home to his wet nurse. She moaned and jerked me closer, gagging me on the fat, chewy protuberance. Then she popped the one thick stem out of my mouth and the other in.

The girls lined up shoulder-to-shoulder, tits-to-tits. And I went excitedly up and down the line, sucking on Holly's right nipple, her left, Stacey's right jutter, her left, back again. Gorging myself on the meaty buds, pink and tan and taut and so very succulent. On my knees in the warm sand, scuttling back and forth like a crazed crab, the girls with their boobs hanging down for my mouth-milking pleasure.

I put my tongue into action, swirling it all around and over Holly's wide areolas, lapping the pink pebble of Stacey's pretty halos. I lifted my leaden arms and grasped their breasts, squeezing, kneading, working the rich, baby-bottom-smooth flesh. As I anxiously licked and lapped at their stiffened nipples, spurred on by their moans of approval.

Eventually, they pulled me to my feet. Then went down into the sand on their knees. They propped their spit-slathered breasts up and offered them to my lower half, smiling encouragingly at me. I had my cock out and splitting cleavage in a flash.

I plunged in between Holly's boobs, prick gliding slippery-smooth up against her breastbone. She promptly sealed her bustage around my dong, and I pumped my hips, fucking her tits. My dick was a blazing iron heat-sealed between mounds of stifling flesh, pistoning back and forth, oiled by the water and perspiration in the girl's golden cleavage.

Then I popped out and in between the beaming Stacey, grabbing her plump hands grasping the sides of her overplump boobs and urgently fucking her tit-tunnel. She met my peek-a-booing purple hood with the tip of her moist, pink tongue, my balls slapping against her breasts, boiling dangerously.

Back and forth I went between the two well-endowed and more-than-willing-to-share women, sliding up and in and churning hard, my cock a numbed slab of meat pile-driving soft and sucking cleavage. I ploughed their tits in a frenzy, frantically groping shuddering breast-meat, sweating rivers and straining every muscle in my body, the sun beating down on the incendiary scene for all the like-minded animals of the forest to see, for all I cared. Smokey with his shovel upside my head couldn't have stopped me just then.

"I'm coming!" I howled, desperately pumping past the point of no return.

"Come on our boobs!" the girls cried, arms and tits trembling like my entire overwrought body.

Semen exploded out of my cap and striped Holly's face, her outstretched tongue. I wrenched my spurting cock out of her cleavage and buried it in Stacey's, painting that girl's lips and chin and chest with hot, sticky jism. I just had enough spunk left to drizzle their upthrust nipples, before toppling over into the shallow water like a felled tree drained of all its sap.

Big Betty was waiting for me in the fire tower; after I'd managed to 'find' the skinny dipping girls' clothing and send them on their way with an official reprimand – and an unofficial request to return the following day, if they possibly could. Big Betty was six-feet-two inches, two-hundred-and-thirty pounds of woman-mountain, bleached blonde and brassy as a tack factory, surly as a she-grizzly. She grimaced at me when I popped my head up into the floor opening.

"Leavin' your post," she grunted, "is a violation of Park Ranger rules."

I climbed to my feet, still looking up at her. "I was just –"

"I know what you were doin'," she growled, tossing the pair of binoculars onto a counter. "You oughta be suspended, or maybe dishonourably discharged from the Service."

"I-I –"

"Stow it, boob! All I wanna know from you is what you're willin' to do to keep me from turnin' you in."

She inhaled a great gulp of air and glared at me, her enormous chest expanding to Herculean proportions. My cock began stirring in response to her challenge, as the buttons on her tunic started popping, one by one, the pressure becoming too much – for them, and me.

Insomnia
by Karyn Winter

He is the most frustrating man I have ever met. His smutty mind, quick wit and dirty laugh can combine to change an innocuous conversation into an innuendo-laden duel which leaves my mind and my cunt engaged. With a curl of his lips and a raised eyebrow he can leave me horny, wet and inarticulate. And the worst thing is: he knows it, and loves seeing me trying to hide it.

Despite how it might sound, I am not utterly obsessed with orgasms. In the bustle of my day-to-day life – lurching through the highs and lows of a job which keeps my mind engaged, juggling responsibilities to friends and family – my sexual predilections often get pushed aside for the wider picture. All work and no play makes Cara a dull girl. Most of the time.

While I will admit that nothing gets me to sleep quite as well as the aftershocks of a good orgasm, there are nights when I fall into bed exhausted from the day without needing to rub myself to completion. But that's because I have the choice. And as the old song says 'you don't know what you've got till it's gone'.

He enjoys torturing me. I know it and usually I like it – I'm firmly of the belief that being tortured by someone you trust makes for fun. But on days like today he's enjoying torturing me more than I am enjoying being tortured and that leaves me frustrated. Very frustrated.

It's been a long day, full of a lot of shit. And while that means this is the kind of blessed adrenaline-fuelled relief I'd have been dreaming of from 9 till 5 if I'd had time for thought,

79

it also means I am desperate for some attention.

Now I know that sounds ridiculous. I'm knelt naked on the bed in front of him, my hands behind my back, pushing my tits up. He is watching me intently as he asks me questions designed to make me blush, to make me wet, to leave me on the back foot trying to figure out how to please him with my answers. When I don't answer quickly enough he slaps my tits and pinches my nipples. I try not to fidget at the onslaught, because when I do the soles of my feet catch my bruised arse and he smiles in satisfaction as I try and hide my reaction to the twinges of pain from the punishment he inflicted with the cane earlier.

He sees everything. More than I'd like. More than I can hide in a million years. He knows how contrary I can be, and it amuses him to see the battle in my eyes between what I want to say and what I can actually bear to force past my dry throat.

Ok. I do have his attention. I just wish it was a bit more … hands on. Every nerve ending is crying out for his touch. His cock. His fingers. His mouth. But so far I'm getting none of that. And with patience definitely not being one of my virtues, waiting is making me almost grind my teeth with frustration. And he can see it and is laughing at me, enjoying the view and the power that he currently holds despite the fact he's just lying against his pillow not even touching me.

"So what should I do with you tonight?"

I hate this question. Hate it. There are so many possibilities. Fucking, sucking, licking, biting, beating (although on second thoughts, I'm not sure my arse can take much more). Images of things we've done before and things I've only dreamed about flash through my mind in quick succession. But what do I say? If I tell him what I'm thinking there's no guarantee he'll do what I've suggested – in fact he's so contrary that the chances are he won't just to keep me off balance. And by telling him I've given him another insight into my mind, which undoubtedly he'll use as a stick to beat me with in some fiendish fashion I can't even begin to think of. Yes, I know I sound paranoid, but as someone wise once said, just because you're paranoid doesn't mean they aren't out to get you.

But the only other possibility, and the one I usually err on the side of, is saying something along the lines of 'I think you should do what you'd like to do'. But that sounds so arse licky that I cringe saying it and have trouble not rolling my eyes while I do. If it works for you then great, but me, well I just feel like a rubbish slutty cliche.

The silence has lengthened while my brain desperately turns over the possibilities trying to come up with something, anything to say.

As I try and form a sentence which might not get me into trouble, he moves from the bed and grabs the butt plug from a drawer.

"Too late." His voice is brusque as he grabs my shoulder and pushes me onto my hands and knees.

He runs his fingernails along the stripes of my arse, as I try not to cry out at the sensation. I bite my lip, and as he spanks me a couple of times on the still-stinging spot my eyes fill with tears. Of course, it's not the only thing flowing, a fact he takes glee in highlighting with a tut, pushing the butt plug into my cunt, easily anointing it with my own juices. He pulls it out with a squelch that sounds like a klaxon pointing out how stupidly horny and desperate I am already and turns his attention to pushing it into my arse, making sure to rest the hand not holding the plug on my poor punished arse cheek, just to ratchet up the sensations zinging through my body making me giddy.

I quiver on my knees as the plug pushes at my hole. Even with the natural lube those first few centimetres are slow and I am tense and difficult to penetrate. He moves his hand for a second to stroke my hair the way you would a panicking horse, and I try to relax myself, to take it, so this game can continue. My deep breathing is helping when a crack echoes across the room, a second before the searing pain knocks me to the bed, my knees giving out at the sheer unexpected pain. In the split second of shock, when the wind is knocked from

81

me and my focus is lost, he shoves the plug up inside me, as far as it will go, further than I think I can take it. I whimper and try to move away, but under his hands, flat on the bed, there is nowhere for me to go. He fills me, stretches me until I can't take any more. I'm assuming my arse is now plugged to his satisfaction, as he's now pushing me over onto my back and – oh this bodes well – he is leaning over me.

"Hands above your head."

I obey, and watch as he rummages through his bedside drawer until he finds two pieces of ribbon to tie my wrists to the headboard with. It looks innocuous enough, the kind of thing you'd buy in a haberdashery, and I make a mental note to avoid wriggling too much and accidentally undoing my bonds. It would kind of spoil the moment.

As he finishes fiddling with the ribbon he looks down to see me staring at his cock, which is swinging pretty much right in front of my face. He smiles. "Did you want something?"

I glower up at him. I want to suck him off. He knows it and I know it.

"I'd like to suck your cock." A pause while he waits for the rest. I sigh. "Please."

My vision is blocked as he pushes himself into my mouth, anchoring his hands into my hair. I love feeling him lengthen in my mouth as I run my tongue along the underside of his cock. Ordinarily I love taking my time to suck him, watching him struggle to keep control for a change. But it's not working like that today. My scalp prickles as he pulls my hair with the force of pushing me onto his cock from below, while his knees pin my shoulders down. All I can do is try to take him without gagging while he fucks my face. I try to move my hands to grab his hips and reassert some control, but I can't move my wrists more than a couple of centimetres, and I feel him thicken even further as I struggle beneath him.

My breathing is ragged, as the only gasps of air I can take are between his relentless thrusts. I can feel tears starting to roll down my cheeks, mingling with my saliva which is running down my chin as I try to lick and suck him to his satisfaction. I begin to adjust to his rhythm, the panicking feeling in my chest that I might choke easing as he abruptly pulls out and straddles me, putting his full weight down on me. He starts to grind against my hips. I cry out in a kind of ecstatic anguish. Every movement pushes the plug pushed further up inside me, the pain from the earlier punishment flying through me with every grind, until I am a whimpering, mewing bundle of sensations. He wanks as he grinds, his eyes flickering from the blush across my tits that signifies I am close to coming, to the pain in my face I try to mask. He runs one hand underneath punished my arse cheek and scratches, hard, along the wounds from earlier and – as I cry out – he comes gushing, huge amounts of hot spunk across my breasts and into my hair. I watch the spectacle greedily, loving seeing how aroused I have made him, and thankful that – finally after hours of teasing and torment – it's almost my turn to get blessed relief.

When he speaks it is the roughened voice of someone who has just come and the first few words are so croaky it takes a second for me to understand.

"When I asked you what I should do with you tonight, you said nothing."

I look up at him, blinking for a moment, trying to focus on the words coming out of his mouth rather than the sensations he is wringing from every part of my body, but I still can't take it in.

"You didn't answer me. I asked you what I should do and you said nothing in response. So tonight that's what you get. Nothing."

He runs a hand down my breast, rolling my nipple between his fingers, tugging and twisting it to punctuate his words.

"I'm going to go to sleep now. And so are you. With your hands still tied like that, just in case you're tempted to bring yourself off during the night." He casually runs a hand between my legs. "You are wet. Slut."

He pulls the duvet up, arranging it carefully so it only covers me from my waist down thus not disturbing the streaks of his spunk drying on my tits. As he settles himself underneath the cover he takes a second to run a finger along the lips of my dripping cunt, making me moan in hope, despair and a guttural horniness which even to my ears sounds desperate.

He chuckles as he snaps the bedside light off. "Sleep well pet."

Having dismissing the ribbons he tied me down with as not that difficult to get out of, an attempt at pulling free of the knots proves that I've got no hope there. My mind is spinning, my juices are running down my inner thighs, I am sticky with his cum, and I lie in the darkness trying to think unsexy thoughts to calm myself through the long night.

I don't know how long I lie there. I am mentally counting off the nine times table in an attempt to switch my brain to something else, when he quickly pushes four fingers of his hand up inside my cunt. I scream, mostly in surprise. The movement is vicious and fleeting, but I am so wet they slip in easily and it's a moment of blessed release, thank fuck, he's going to let me come, he was bluffing, just wondering if he could make me cry with frustration. Make me beg.

My whole body is on alert once more. Waiting, yearning for the next touch. My ears are straining to hear his movement, my eyes staring into the darkness to glimpse some clue of what he is doing. The silence lengthens. He idly pats my breast as he turns over, gathers up some duvet and gets himself comfortable on his side of the bed.

"I get so bored when I wake at night with my insomnia. I'll probably just play with you for a bit if I can't sleep. Stop me if it bothers you." I can hear the smile in his voice. "Oh. You can't. Oh well. You'll get to come eventually. Just not tonight."

As his breathing slows, and he goes back to sleep, I stare at the chink of street light coming in through the curtains, willing it to get brighter and for day to come, because I know there will be no sleep for me tonight.

There are nights when I fall into bed exhausted from the

day without needing to rub myself to completion. But as I lie in the darkness, listening to him sleep, the very fact that I can't come means that my entire being is focused on the pulse between my legs, the plug up my arse and my desperate need to orgasm.

He is the most frustrating man I have ever met. And I mean that literally.

Candle Light
by January James

Tuesday Troy stood at her large bedroom window eagerly awaiting the first glimpse of her husband's car pulling into the driveway. She was so excited she panted a little. She'd never done anything so daring before. She envisaged the look on Patrick's handsome face when he saw her. His soft blue eyes would darken in pleasure and he'd give her that little boy smile which melted her heart every time.

He was so gentle and patient, giving her the support she'd needed to start her own candle-making business. He understood how much she'd hated corporate America and how long this business had been in her heart. This was her baby and like most husbands he'd been pushed to the side once it was born. He rarely complained though Tuesday knew he hated the long hours she spent at her store, the networking trips she took all over the country and giving up his precious weekends to browse flea markets while she blissfully hunted unique candle holders. This was her way of saying thank you.

Her heart skipped a few beats as headlights illuminated the driveway. She hurried from the window and positioned herself in the lotus position among the colourful pillows she'd scattered on the floor. She closed her eyes and imagined him opening the front door, seeing the rose petals leading up the stairs and that smile lighting up his face. He'd take of his jacket and shoes. By the time he reached their bedroom he'd be mostly naked and aroused. She smiled. Poor guy hadn't had any in such a long time.

She heard his heavy breathing and opened her eyes. He

stood in the door in just his boxer briefs and a burning in his eyes. She'd never loved or wanted him more than she did in that moment.

"Welcome home, darling," she cooed.

"If I'd known this is what was waiting for me I'd have left the bar hours ago." He stared at her. "God, you're beautiful. What is that you have written on your body?"

Tuesday held out one elegant hand. "Come sit with me."

When Patrick removed his underwear her breath stopped painfully in her throat. How had she managed to live for weeks without that beautiful piece of male craftsmanship? She used to crave the impressive length, his thickness filling her with rock hard heat.

Patrick stood in front of her for a second and she rubbed her face against his cock, inhaling his scent and luxuriating in the feel of him. As she filled her lungs with his essence her bones seemed to melt into molten larva. She ached with her need for him. He hardened against her skin. Gazing longingly up at him she saw his eyes were wild and crazy with desire. She loved the power she had over him, how she could turn him to mush while his cock transformed into granite. She was tempted to take him into her mouth. Her mouth watered begging her for one taste, just to feel him throbbing against the delicacy of her tongue.

Patrick caressed the back of her head, silently begging her for what they both wanted. But she didn't want him coming so soon. He'd gone without for so long that it wouldn't take much for him to explode. She wasn't sure she possessed the willpower and groaned in frustration. But she managed to control herself, instead grasping his hands and pulling him down beside her.

Patrick looked around the room. "I can't believe you did all this."

She'd decorated the room with candles and sheer fabric draped over the bedposts and lamps. She'd also hung four large erotic art pencil drawings she'd found on a solo trip to the flea market.

Patrick crossed his legs and Tuesday sat in his lap, wrapping her hands around his waist and crossing her legs around his hips. Patrick placed one had on her lower back and the other on her hip. His cock nestled against her pussy and behind. Moving ever so slightly, she rubbed against him.

He started examining the writings on her chest.

"I'm sorry I've been so preoccupied with business lately," she said.

"It's understandable. Starting a business is not easy."

"But neither is being married so I have to work on both."

Patrick smiled. "Yeah, you're working on me alright, baby. Your body looks amazing."

"It's chocolate body paint and some of my feelings," she explained.

He caressed her collar bone. "So you want to be kissed here." His lips glided over the area. "And caressed here." He caressed her left breast cupping its fullness in his hand.

Tuesday moaned. It felt so good having his hands on her body. Each instruction took her to a new level of delight. When he finally kissed her lips he tasted of chocolate and desire. His lips went from soft to hard in an instant. She held on to his tongue, savagely sucking him then desperately trying to get to the back of his throat. She couldn't get enough of him, couldn't get close enough. His mouth was wet and she dived deep seeking sweetness and release. Her pussy creamed and throbbed, her essence leaking out on his rapidly expanding cock.

Patrick pulled his mouth away from hers with a loud moan. He reached between them, took his cock, and placed it between her lips. He rubbed the head against her clit while staring into her dark brown eyes. She held his gaze feeling the energy from his body flow into hers. She inhaled when he exhaled. They barely moved but their centre, where their bodies joined, crackled with electricity. She arched her hips and leaned into him, rubbing her breasts against his smooth chest. Her body begged her to let go, to end the sweet torture, and bask in the warmth of blessed release. But she wanted to hold on to the tension, allowing it to build until the choice of when she came wasn't hers to control any more.

As if he read her mind Patrick lifted his cock away from her. "I have a feeling you have more surprises in store for me tonight," he said.

Tuesday smiled. "I wanted us to try some of my new candles." She reached over to a basket she'd conveniently placed near the pillows and selected one of her massage candles and a lighter. As she lit the candle she noted the look of concern on Patrick's face.

She placed the candle on the floor and tried to assuage his fears. "The wax will melt into a massage oil. It's a low burning soy candle so you won't get burned – well maybe a little but trust me, it will hurt so good."

She pushed him back onto the pillows and lifted herself high enough for him to stretch out his legs.

He sighed in relief then said. "I love this new take-charge side of you. I never knew you had a fetish for hot wax."

"There are a lot of things you still don't know about me but it's nice to know you trust me to take care of you."

While they waited for the wax to melt Patrick sat up and tweaked her nipples.

"You've never looked more beautiful than you do in this moment. You look like a goddess to me."

Tuesday threw back her head and laughed. She felt like a goddess upon her adoring stallion. Patrick started licking the chocolate from her body, creating swirls with his tongue. Tuesday sighed blissfully, slowly bending backwards until her head touched the floor. Patrick reached under her supporting his weight with one hand. She reached up and took his feet in her hands.

Tuesday felt open and vulnerable. Her stomach muscles twitched as Patrick circled her navel with his tongue. His free hand moved between her thighs, gently rubbing the outer lips as if seeking permission to enter.

"Yesss," she expelled on a long breath.

Jubilantly his fingers slipped in, finding and stroking that little nubbin of hard flesh for just a second- a tease really, before moving to the inner lips. He seduced her clit, tempting it with a touch, making it beg by moving away. Tuesday extended her legs and dug her heels into the carpet, lifting her hips, begging him to taste her.

Patrick stared at her offering, admiring its perfection. She was always smooth, with his name tattooed just below her bikini line. The little minx had enjoyed the pain. He hadn't enjoyed having her name etched into his crotch but she was worth every second of pain. He ran his tongue over his suddenly dry lips and imagined it was the wet lips inches from his face.

But she wasn't quite ready. This was the game they liked to play, pushing each other to the limits of endurance.

"I think that candle is ready now," he said in a voice so thick with desire he didn't even recognize it as his own.

Tuesday sat back down on his lap. She was glad he'd had the self-control to stop but her frustration was making her crazy. She didn't know how much more she could stand.

She reached for the candle. "Heat on skin can be extremely sensual," she explained as she held the candle high enough over her chest so it would have a little time to cool before splattering onto her skin. When it did she growled, closing her eyes to feel its full impact. She rubbed the warm oil across her breasts. "Oh God, this feels so good."

Patrick's hand joined hers, massaging the oil into her skin. The heat seemed to seep into her pores, travelling through her body down to her pussy.

"Lay back, you have to feel this," she whispered.

Patrick lay reclined on the pillows as she raised the candle above him. He watched the oil coming towards him and held his breath. It hit his chest smoothly, running in rivulets down to his flat stomach. The hint of pain jolted his senses into overdrive. He moaned at the unexpected pleasure as Tuesday rubbed the oil into him.

"When you get used to this we can move on to hotter stuff," she promised.

91

"Are you going to reveal all of your sexual secrets before you met me?" he asked.

Tuesday's smile was a little nostalgic. "There really isn't much to tell. I spent more time alone than with partners. I started making candles. One day I made a penis candle and I was converted. I've never looked at wax the same way since."

"Now thanks to you I won't either."

Patrick sat up and pushed her back onto the floor. He reached for the penis shaped candle and blew out the flame. He rubbed the wick and tip with his hand, making sure it was warm but not hot. Tuesday placed her feet on his chest and opened her legs. Patrick placed the candle directly on her clit. She screamed and dug her nails into the carpet. It was so unbelievably erotic she broke out in sweat. As he moved the big candle against her pussy she finally reached the point of no return. She surrendered herself, body, mind, and soul to the ultimate pleasure.

She never made a sound, she just shook like a woman possessed. She pushed against Patrick's strong chest, her hips slapped against his lap and she bit down so hard on her bottom lip she tasted blood.

Patrick placed the candle on the ground and cupped her pussy as she gently came back down to earth. They were silent for a few minutes as she tried to get air into her lungs. Finally she opened her eyes and smiled up at him.

Patrick's eyes were soft. "Remember earlier when I said you've never looked more beautiful? I was wrong because you've never been more beautiful than you were just now. You were simply poetry in motion."

Tuesday blushed. "God, you know just what to say to get yourself laid."

Patrick smiled. "So it's that time now?" he reached down and caressed his cock.

Hunger quickly replaced the glow of her orgasm. She sat up and placed her hips above Patrick's erection then gently slid down its length. Her body accepted him gleefully. Slowly she started dancing, her hips moving in graceful patterns. She placed her hands on his chest and bent forward, elongating their strokes. Patrick pushed up into her, his hardness slamming into her softness savagely. He was so thick and driving so deeply it hurt. In an effort to relax the pressure Tuesday locked her legs around Patrick's waist and leaned back. Sensing her need Patrick folded his legs under him and grabbed her forearms. She followed his lead. Their entwined hands allowed them to bend backwards while lessening the power of their thrusts.

While their arms remained tense and their hips moved frantically, their upper bodies appeared to be floating. Tuesday felt as if she were flying through soft clouds in a rainbow of colours. Their heavy breathing sounded heavier in the quiet room. Their bodies glistened with sweat from the heat of the candles and their erotic dance.

Their positions didn't alleviate the pain for long. There was no way to avoid the ache of such an intense desire. Tuesday released his hands, returning to her original position taking him deep inside her. She slammed down on him, welcoming the jolt to her body and senses. She started hissing then groaning as Patrick reached down and started rubbing her clit.

She came first, her muscles tightening even more around him as she shuddered and cried out his name. Knowing she was taken care of, Patrick exploded, filling her with liquid heat. Tuesday slumped on top of him and linked her arms around his neck.

Patrick kissed the top of her head. "I think I'm ready for some of that hotter stuff you promised."

Tuesday looked up at him in delight. "I knew you'd like it. I should've shared this with you a long time ago."

He caressed her shoulders. "You don't have to be afraid to share anything with me, sexual or otherwise. Especially something as amazing as this."

She wriggled her hips against his. "Do you have any secrets that I need to know?"

Patrick's smile was a little deviant. "Maybe. You'll just have to wait and see. Right now let's just concentrate on getting hot."

At this point each candle held a little pool of hot ecstasy. She poured them into a miniature, vintage tea pot, also a flea market find, and placed it on an electric warmer. It would keep the wax melted long enough for them to have fun.

"I'll go first." Tuesday stretched out on her stomach and pulled her long black hair away from her neck and back. "Now carefully pour a trail from my neck down to my hips," she instructed. "And I don't mind if you get a little carried away. I can take the heat."

"Man I like this new side of you," Patrick said happily as he held the teapot above the slim back. He poured slowly while moving the pot down her back, leaving a trail of heat. Tuesday moaned but didn't flinch. The sensation of liquid heat on bare skin was exquisite.

"Again, please do it again," she cried softly.

Patrick followed up with another trail this time dropping a few drips between her spread thighs. She turned over onto her back. She loved feeling the congealed wax pressing into her skin. "Now do my nipples."

Patrick replaced the empty pot and lit a fresh candle. When the liquid started melting he angled it directing the wax to her large areola. Her back arched when fire met skin. Her fingers moved between her legs and she played with herself while he administered heat to her breasts. She gave a high piercing whimper and in a second she came.

She looked up at Patrick and smiled. "Wouldn't you like to know what that feels like."

"I think I'm gonna right now." He handed her the candle and stretched out on his back. He had an eager grin on his face that reminded Tuesday of a little boy on Christmas morning. God, how she loved him!

She knelt beside him and aimed the wax towards his nipple. He didn't say anything at first. He was too busy trying to analyze the sensations he was experiencing. But when he allowed his mind to simply surrender he connected with a part of himself straddling the thin line between pleasure and pain.

When Tuesday ran a stream of wax down the length of his cock, his moan stopped halfway in his throat. The sensitive skin, thinned from stretching to accommodate his erection, throbbed with excitement. As the wax congealed she peeled it away pulling little fine hairs with it.

"Oh shit, that hurts so good! Hurt me again, baby," he growled out.

Tuesday played with him taking him to the brink of his control before putting aside the candle and laying down next to him. She placed one leg over him and lifted her hips slightly for him to enter her. Patrick grabbed her hips. This time their dance was gentle. She caressed his head as they moved together. He alternated his caresses between her hips and breasts. They gazed into each other's eyes and talked like they hadn't since their honeymoon.

So much of their conversations lately had read like to-do lists. When they were dating her smile had been a topic of conversation, the way he looked in his jeans had given her butterflies.

Tuesday knew they couldn't live in a bubble blissfully tucked away from real life but they needed more moments like this, to talk about sweet nothings which really meant so much.

Their climax was more of a gentle wave filling them with warmth but still leaving them breathless and basking in the glow of the candle lights.

Meeting Mister M
by Evalina Frances

He's not a total stranger.

For the hundredth time I repeat this to myself as I move one station closer to my destination. The rocking rumble of the tube train is both calming and ominous. The butterflies in my stomach fall quiet then erupt into a mass of fluttering each time the doors open and then clamp shut.

I look at my reflection in the darkened window opposite. My long messy bob is tamed in a knot at the base of my neck, leaving a curtain of dark fringe from under which my green eyes seductively peep. The fitted white blouse unbuttoned, showing more than a hint of the black bra that barely contains my ample cleavage, and it clings perfectly, accentuating my waist. A neat black skirt skims my hips and stops just below my knee so that my calves, dressed in the sheerest of stockings, looked toned and tanned all the way to my 4 inch giraffe print heels.

I smile at the girl that stares back at me from the glass, even more pleased with myself when I think of what is hidden beneath my outfit. It's all about the lingerie for *Mister M*.

I'm here, my stop. I stand, grab my bag and hop onto the platform. My echoing heels click time with my repeated mantra …

He's not a total stranger. He's not a total stranger.

We've known each other for some time. Drawn to a site of erotic writings, I couldn't contain my curiosity from peeking at pictures of its members. *Mister M* had stood out immediately. Unlike the other faceless, gratuitous shots of cocks in various states of arousal, his were interesting, cheeky and oh so sexy! Some stripping in a suit, others in jeans without boxers, wrapped only in a white sheet or naughtily under the desk at work they had made me smile as well as making my pussy wet.

Uncharacteristically, I soon posted some of my own and it seemed my pictures had the same effect on *Mister M*. We started chatting and before long progressed to webcams. I lacked the hardware so swapped his spare camera for a pair of my panties which I had misted in just a hint of my perfume, the same perfume I wore today. The first time I heard him call me his 'good girl' in my headphones, a jolt of desire ran through my body, ending up in a slippery mess between my legs. It was addictive and electric – cyber sex that rivalled the real thing.

It was inevitable we would meet.

Reaching the top of the stairs I step out into the early summer sunshine. I love London at this time of year and the most obvious place to meet was right in its heart, Trafalgar Square. We'd arranged just outside the National Gallery but now, as the butterflies twisted themselves into a frenzy in my belly, I feel a sharp stab of nerves.

Hanging back from the spot we'd agreed, but keeping it in clear view, I pull out my phone. I'll call, and watch him waiting. Make sure I really want this before I commit.

It only rings twice. He answers.

'Hey D, where are you?' The voice I know so well from my fantasies licks at my ear and my knees buckle.

I can't see him where he should be standing.

'I'm here, M.' I reply, my eyes frantically scanning the stone steps of the gallery in case he is hidden in the crowd. 'I can't see you.'

My heart races, I can't stand still. I need to see him first.

'Well I'm right where I said I'd be.'

My searching is fruitless but he sounds close.

'Where exactly?' I ask. 'What can you see?'

'You.'

I feel a hand on my shoulder and hear a phone snap shut.

For a second I am too scared to look, still foolishly holding the phone to my ear. Taking a deep breath I begin to turn on my heel.

The moment I see his eyes, sparkling blue and green, I realise it is futile to resist. Without a word his hand is on the back of my neck and he kisses me full and hard, his other hand firm on the small of my back, pulling me into him. I surrender totally to the most passionate encounter of my life. A massive surge of adrenalin burns through every pore as his tongue investigates mine and his lips grind into me.

The tips of his fingers teasingly slide under the hem of my blouse and brush my back. His touch on my bare skin causes my pussy to tighten and I know if he hadn't held me, I would dissolve into a pool on the pavement. My hands grasp at his strong shoulder, desperately wanting to feel the smooth, warm skin underneath.

I feel his mouth break into a smile and as he pulls back, he gently grips on my bottom lip with his teeth. I giggle. I can't help it, casting my eyes downwards and instantly back up to his face, the face I know so well from a tiny window on my laptop screen. Here, in the sunlight I notice the red in his thick hair and don't stop my hand as it reaches up to touch it. My eyes never leave his face.

He'd listened when I said I liked stubble and the growth on his chin holds promise of a grazing between my thighs that I can't wait to experience. I giggle again and as his laugh joins mine, I notice what perfect teeth he has.

'Want to see my room?' he enquires, and anticipating my answer takes my hand in his and leads me out of the hustle and bustle of the square.

I walk beside him, my heels causing my hips to sway and bump into his with each stride. Our bodies are so close that I can smell his cleanly soaped skin and a vision of him in a steamy shower causes me to wobble slightly. Our fingers hang together like tangled vines, as though we have been holding hands for years. Silently we walk for a few minutes until we reach the entrance to a hotel, grander than I had expected. The doorman welcomes us as we pass and smiles politely. The lobby is smart, large and anonymous – perfect for our purpose. Casually he hits the button for the lift. I watch his fingers and long to feel them disappearing inside me.

The doors open with a 'ding' and we step inside. Without waiting for them to fully close, I twist and kiss him, hungry to taste his mouth again. He steps back as I devour him, our teeth clash and my hips pin him to the wall, the buckle of his belt digging into my soft stomach. There is no denying how excited he is through the crotch of his Levis, the jeans from the photos I so admire, and I wonder if he is naked inside them. I have to fight against touching his cock and instead place my hands on his chest, the hair within his cool cotton shirt surrounds his hard nipples and a rush shoots through me ending in a soaking spasm between my legs.

I moan words, broken between kisses.

'I … want … you … inside … me …'

The lift stops and he leads me along the corridor to the room, trailing his fingertips around my waist, brushing against the underside of my breasts as he opens the door. We only manage a couple of steps inside before my back is against the wall, his weight deliciously holding me there. His hands push my wrists high above my head as his lips meet mine once more. I eagerly accept, but move my kisses from his lips to nuzzle into him. My tongue licks his neck and he moans as I knew he would. I laugh and, as my teeth nip his ear, he flips me round so suddenly I gasp as my face is pushed against the door frame.

In a second my skirt is around my waist, his hands run up my thighs to savour the silky tops of my stockings, and then onto naked flesh as he holds me firm. Fingertips caress the sheer fabric of my underwear and a trickle of anticipation escapes my pussy, running down the inside of my thigh and onto his hand. He pauses briefly to lick it from his fingers then pulls my panties to the side and without hesitation, forces two fingers deep inside me. I groan as I feel his hot breath on the back of my neck, his teeth grazing as he kisses. His free hand works itself between my body and the wall, grabbing at my overflowing breasts. His cock, fully erect within his jeans, is hard against my arse and as I feel my sex begin to spasm, he stops.

I want to stamp my heel in frustration but no sooner do I catch my breath than he shoves me face down on the bed. The sound of his belt sliding through the buckle fills me with sweet expectancy, he unzips his fly and I raise myself up to him. I know his buzz is to fuck with lingerie on and as I feel his fingers stroke my silky, sodden panties I know he is relishing the view.

It takes all my self-control not to orgasm.

I turn my head to look just as he smears his precum around the red head of his solid cock with the same fingers that had been buried in me. I stare at the member I have adored during our online liaisons and the thought that it will soon be pounding into me almost tips me over the edge again. He takes his sticky fingers and leaning forward, slips them into my mouth. I lap at the combination of our juices, watching as he tears into a condom wrapper with his teeth, slipping it over his throbbing cock. I start to purr as he slowly rubs the red head of his dick on my swollen clit, the heat from it sensational against my dripping flesh.

I ache for him. I cannot wait.

'Fuck me, Mister M!' I demand, shuddering as he obeys and hammers himself into me, deeper than I have ever known before.

His fingers dig into my pale skin as he fucks me furiously, guaranteeing bruised souvenirs of our first encounter. Within a few thrusts I succumb entirely to the pulsating waves inside me, squirting all over his throbbing cock and biting down on the bed to stop myself from screaming. He pulls out and I turn onto my back, reaching down to touch myself as I look into his beautiful eyes, never dropping my gaze as he groans, spraying thick drops of spunk all over my burning pussy.

'Good girl' he whispers down at me, still wanking proudly.

'You're a good girl.'

Those words have fuelled my dreams since we first met and now, hearing them for real, a shudder of pure satisfaction rocks my body. I laugh and smear his stickiness all around my clit, almost too sensitive to touch. He flops on the bed beside me, his eyes dazzling, laughing too.

Over his shoulder I notice the bedside clock. It is only 30 minutes since we met in the bright daylight of the most public place in London and yet here we are, just yards away and acquainted in the most intimate way. It feels as though I have known him for a lifetime. I think back to my trepidation on the Tube train and wonder what I had ever been worried about.

He is certainly no longer a stranger – and we still have the rest of the night.

Our lips touch again, softly this time, savouring every second as though we were born to explore each other. My eyes are closed but I know he is grinning once more through his kiss.

Blissfully, I wrap my arms around him and allow myself to melt.

Lisa's Lessons
by Izzy French

I knew Martin was gay, of course, probably before he did. So it came as no surprise when he came out to me the day he left for college. It was a relief in fact. The pretence we'd been keeping up till then was beginning to show the cracks. And at least now we could have a more open and honest relationship, or so I hoped.

"Just have fun, son," I said as I kissed him goodbye. "Be careful and work hard."

I didn't see him for a couple of months after that. Too much partying, I imagined. I had to admit to being the teensiest bit jealous. I'd had Martin young, out of wedlock, as my mum called it. There'd always been just the two of us, and we'd been close and spent a lot of time together. I'd tried to kick-start my social life when Martin was about a year old, but it had been difficult to be a single mother and get out a lot. I did manage the odd singles club, or speed dating session with my best friend Clare, but besides the occasional dinner date and quick, often unsatisfying, fumble they didn't amount to much. And now Martin had left home I felt too young to give up on the idea of partying myself, and wished I could join him. Now doubt his new social life was a blast. But what eighteen-year-old gay man would want to drag his mum along to a club, and have her cramp his style? Not many, I'm sure. And I missed him too. We got on so well together. Had a laugh and a giggle, and a cry too over soppy films. We had our moments like all mothers and sons, but they were rare. And I'd been really looking forward to his first visit home, after a couple of

103

months away. He arrived early on a Friday evening.

"Hi, Mum, hope you don't mind but Tom's come to stay for a couple of nights."

I looked at Tom as he followed Martin into the kitchen. How could I mind? He was gorgeous. Tall, slim, a wild mop of blond curls and a goofy smile. Eye candy for the middle-youth woman, that was for sure. And, of course, almost certainly gay. And not only gay, but chances were high that he was my son's boyfriend, the first he'd ever brought home. This was going to be a steep learning curve. What was the etiquette around that? Did I offer to make them up the spare bedroom, the one next to mine? And, more importantly, the one with the double bed with squeaky springs, so if there was any nocturnal activity I would hear everything. Or did I put them in Martin's bedroom, in the bunk beds? He'd been used to sharing his room with his mate Paul, when they'd dossed down here after working on their A-level projects. Maybe that's what he'd prefer to do with Tom, share the bunks. Carry on with a tradition. And, though I had no problem with Martin being gay, and bringing home a boyfriend, it might spare all our blushes, for the first visit at least. I just wanted Martin to be safe and happy. Isn't that what every mother wants for her son? Oh, and to be looked after and cared for. I wondered if Tom was the looking after and caring for type.

"Hello, Mrs Bateman, lovely to meet you."

He shook my hand. I warmed to his manner immediately. And I couldn't stop myself feel a twinge of jealousy. And that felt strange, feeling jealous of my son's luck.

"Lisa, please. Mrs Bateman makes me feel about 70. And anyway, I'm not, Mrs that is. Cup of tea? Beer?"

"A beer would be great, Lisa. Thanks."

And the evening went swimmingly from then on. I cooked for them, we sat round the table and ate, drank beer and red wine, gossiped and laughed. Tom's smile was completely infectious, and it was good to have my house reverberate with the sound of men. It felt like he was flirting with me, which felt good, though I was conscious of what Martin would feel.

104

He didn't seem to notice. Or mind. It was the best time I'd had in ages.

"Cool, Mum," Martin said when I told him about my suggested sleeping arrangements.

When I finally made it downstairs the next morning, feeling a little groggy from the wine, Martin had left me a note to say he'd popped round to visit an old school friend, Paul, who was home that week too. He said not to worry about Tom. He'd probably have a lie-in and work on some college stuff until Tom got back.

"Morning, Lisa." Tom's voice took me by surprise. It sounded deeper, like he'd just got out of bed, which, by the look of him, was the case. His hair was unbrushed and he wore a tight T-shirt and jeans that fell around his slim hips, exposing a line of dark hair leading down to his groin. I looked, then looked away, blushing.

"Cup of tea?" I asked, brightly. I was still in my dressing gown, which I pulled more tightly round me, as I was naked underneath. It didn't generally matter what I wore around the house, as these days there was rarely anyone to see. Not that Tom would be interested in me. Not only was I nearly twice his age, but he was also probably far more interested in my son.

"Thanks, let me get it." He came closer and his hand brushed over mine as he reached for the kettle. This one touch sent a tingle throughout my whole body. I must be starved of affection, I thought, if this is how I react to a brief encounter over a kettle. As I reached up to the cupboard I felt my breasts rub against the silk of my dressing gown, and I caught Tom's eye. He was gazing at the curve of my breasts, I was sure. The 'v' of my dressing gown deepened as I placed two cups on the side, and I crossed my hands across my chest to cover myself up. Tom was close to me. I breathed in deeply, inhaling the scent of him. Not the heavy cologne, mixed with whisky, of the men I met at singles club. But the sharp and sweet smell of a young man just out of bed. I admitted to myself now just how much I wanted him. He reached forwards and brushed my

105

hair back, placing his hand gently under my chin and bringing my eyes up to meet his. He was a foot taller than me at least.

"Me and Martin." His voice trailed away and his fingers grazed over my cheek.

"Yes," I replied.

"We're just friends you know. Good friends. But just friends. I like girls. Well, women."

I just nodded. And then he leant down and kissed me. It was just the lightest touch of a kiss at first. Tentative. I imagine he was uncertain, waiting for my response. So I returned his kiss, opened my mouth to him. The taste of him was wonderful. Sweet like his scent. We stood and kissed in the kitchen for an age, like teenagers, which I guess he was. It felt so good. Warmth radiated through my body and we moved closer together. I felt his body press against mine. I laid my hands on his hips. He was angular and firm. No soft edges to him. He pulled away. I felt momentarily disappointed. Had he changed his mind? Did he think he'd made a mistake? Oh, God, how awful would that be? Not least, now because I was anticipating and fantasizing about what would happen next.

"I definitely like women," he whispered softly. "Women just like you. May I?" He reached for my dressing gown belt, which was tied into a loose bow.

"Yes, please do." In one deft movement he undid the bow and pulled my gown apart, so it was just resting on my shoulders, exposing my body to him. My instinct was to cover up, cross my legs and pull my hands across my body. But I resisted.

"You're beautiful." His fingers traced imaginary lines down my body from my neck, across my breasts and stomach, to the top of my thighs. Kissing me again, he then nuzzled into my neck, taking the weight of my breasts in his hands. My nipples were hard now, responding to his touch. He twisted and turned them gently between his fingers, then reached down to kiss them. Every possible nerve ending responded as he licked and sucked on my nipples and breasts. He tongue circled each nipple, slowly at first, then more quickly. He licked each areole, then blew gently, his breath feeling cool against my wet skin. I had to shake myself mentally. Was this bliss really happening? How could this experience be so different from the selfish fumbles of my more recent encounters? I pushed these thoughts from my mind, and decided to enjoy this moment for what it was. Pure pleasure. I would surrender myself and enjoy. As if he sensed this, Martin ran his hands over the curve of my hips and tangled his fingers first in my pubic hair, then delved deeper into the folds between my legs. My hands had rested on his shoulders until this moment. But if he was to explore me so deeply, then why couldn't I? It was many years since I'd run my hands over the body of a fit young eighteen-year old. And it felt good. His hips were narrow. His skin was smooth. I ran my hands around the waistband of his low-slung jeans. And he gasped. Taking this as encouragement, I undid the buttons and peeled them away. He wore nothing under his jeans, and his cock was hard. I took it between my hands and began to caress him, pulling gently at his foreskin, and reaching into his jeans to cup his balls, which I could feel tighten at my touch.

"Wait," he said. Again, for a moment, I anticipated disappointment, but he was just pulling off his jeans and T-shirt, then my gown and throwing them into the corner of the kitchen. We stood facing one another now, both naked, and both extremely aroused. Taking the initiative I knelt in front of him, and took his cock into my mouth. His hands brushed though my hair, encouraging my. His cock filled my mouth as I sucked him rhythmically, my tongue encircling him. I could hear him groan, and began to feel him thrust into my mouth, and I expected him to come now, and I was ready to swallow his sweet juices.

"No, wait, I want us to come together." He pulled his cock from my mouth and lifted me up, kissing me again, tasting himself on my lips. Putting his hands around my waist he lifted me onto the table, sitting me on the edge, and parting my legs. Then it was his turn to kneel in front of me. I leant back, exposing my cunt to him. At first he just looked, caressing my inner thighs as he did so. Then he parted the folds of my labia with his fingers, gently but insistently, and found my clitoris. His touch was exquisite. I was wet with excitement now.

"Fuck me," I pleaded.

"Soon," he replied, then buried his mouth into my cunt, his tongue inside me at first, then twisting and turning my clitoris, sending shudders through me. He pushed one hand into me, and I could feel myself clench and release around it. I knew I was close to coming now, to losing control. But there was nothing I could do. Looking down I could see he was tugging on his cock with his free hand, bringing pearls of cum to the tip. I wanted that cock inside me now, pushing my folds to the limit. He sensed my need, gave my clitoris one last suck, which almost made me explode with desire and pleasure then stood in front of me, his beautiful cock nudging at my cunt.

"Ready?" He asked, knowing I was. My body pulsed with wanting him, and all I could do was part my legs further and offer my cunt to him in reply. At first he nudged and teased the entrance, releasing my juices, ensuring a smooth passage. The sensation was so sweet as his cock pushed into me, slowly but firmly. I opened up to him as he reached deeper and deeper into me. Then he began to thrust and I matched his rhythm as his fingers circled my clitoris again. The waves of no-going-back desire soon overcame me and I cried out with the pleasure of my release as I felt my cunt pulse around his cock, and, in turn, felt him reach his climax and thrust his juices deep into me. My pleasure seemed endless, as did his. When he finally pulled away, I reached down to my cunt, then brought my fingers to my mouth, savouring the sweet and salty taste of our inter-mingled juices. He pulled me towards him, and held me close for an age, kissing my hair, stroking his hands down my back. I showered his chest with tiny kisses, and I could feel his cock harden against my thigh. The joys of a younger man, I thought, as I dropped to my knees again, this time determined to satisfy him with my mouth. And this time he allowed me.

Martin arrived home shortly after I'd pulled my dressing

gown on and re-tied the bow, and Tom had tugged on his jeans and T-shirt.

"Cup of tea, Martin?" I offered him, as we all sat around the table, my chair next to Tom's. I pulled my eyes away from Tom, and glanced at my son. Martin's eyes were shining and his lips looked bruised, somehow. Then I remembered he'd been to see Paul that morning, and the truth dawned on me.

"Great, Mum. Hey it was good to catch up with Paul this morning. Mind if I go out with him tonight? Will you two be OK on your own?"

I felt Tom's hand run up my thigh and across my stomach, sending desire shoot through me.

"We'll be fine, Martin. Won't we, Tom? Don't worry about us."

"Yeah, Martin, you go out and have fun. Everything will be taken care of here."

When Penny Met Daniel
by Judith Roycroft

When Penny opened her eyes she was flat on her back, staring up at a man she'd only ever seen the likes of in her raunchiest dreams.

Then he went and spoilt it all by sneering.

"What are you doing in that archaic gear?"

Penny glanced down at her lemony crop-top and muslin skirt that stuck to her thighs like clingwrap.

"I beg your pardon? I had to fight my girlfriend for these in the Op shop only yesterday."

Eyeing the amazing hunk spread-eagled above, Penny decided it was a pity he wasn't smiling. Most men did when their gaze lingered on her body, but this guy acted totally immune to her considerable charms.

She stuck out her hand. "Give us a heave up, could you?"

The man stayed planted where he was.

"Charming, I'm sure," Penny sniffed, jumping to her feet without his help.

He stared coldly at her. "Women must not flaunt their breasts."

Tolerant of other people's opinions, Penny, in this instance, decided he'd gone too far.

So she wasn't wearing a bra.

So her breasts jiggled enticingly at the slightest movement.

But flaunting them? Never! At least, not at this moment.

"You must be from another planet, boyo, if you think I'm

111

parading anything."

"I am from planet Earth."

Penny stared at him. He appeared normal, yet it was unreal, this wacky exchange.

"That makes two of us," she muttered, glancing round curiously. Moments ago her bare feet were dreamily caressing her parents' dew-sprinkled lawn. Now rocks were jabbing the tender underflesh. So, what was *he* doing in this deserted place?

What was going on here? Her young sister had been by her side and now she'd vanished. They'd been admiring a rainbow that arced its way gracefully across the silvery-grey sky. For a moment Penny had felt herself floating ...

"Oh, my God! I'm somewhere else!" There was a clear blue sky and not a rainbow in sight.

The hunk still hovered and the manner in which his gaze continued to skip over her was more puzzling than assessing.

The skyline was unfamiliar. "What city is this?" asked Penny.

The guy frowned at her, as though she'd lost her marbles. "New York."

Relieved, Penny studied her companion. Dressed in a sexy black trench coat and respectable jeans – he could have done with a size or three smaller she noted – he didn't look all that strange, but there was a formality to his speech, which sounded odd. And he'd disparaged her clothes. God, they weren't *that* old! Besides, it was funky to wear vintage clothes.

She took a big breath. Crisp, clean air; not the usual smell of exhaust and myriad odours with which she was familiar. New York he'd said. It wasn't quite *her* New York.

"What year is this?" she asked, suddenly suspicious. If he thought her question peculiar, he refrained from commenting.

"The year 2097."

"Shite!" Penny yelped. "I've done a spot of time travel." Still, not one to miss out, and considering the man was positively delectable, Penny took his hand, deciding to make the most of this stellar opportunity. "How about a tour of 2097 then, sweetie?"

Immediately he shook free. "It is forbidden to connect with female flesh."

"Oh. What do you do for pleasure?" she asked slyly, sidling up to him.

When he moved smartly away it didn't faze Penny. She was expecting it.

"It has been banned. It is counter-productive."

"Holy hell!" Penny nibbled her lower lip. She wouldn't have chosen this period if she'd had any say in the matter. "Look. Do you have to sound like a bloody robot every time you speak?"

"You must get off the streets. You will be arrested. Women must cover themselves."

Penny rolled her eyes. "This isn't the Middle East, is it?"

He gave a derisive snort. "Of course not. I have already told you this is New York."

"Oh, yeah. Well, relax, Max. Just trying to come to terms with all this."

"My name is Daniel."

"Thank God for that! I expected to hear you spout something like Zentor. Or Zaboo. Even Xeno-something."

"I'm not from outer space," he rebuked.

Penny wisely decided to let that ride.

"Give us a tour, will you?"

Looking none too happy, Daniel nevertheless turned, and she followed. "Can I walk beside you?"

"No."

They rounded a corner and Penny gaped. "Holy hell!" The once familiar landmarks of old New York were rubble and, in their stead, giant chrome buildings saluted the skyline. As they approached an unshaded window at street level, Penny observed several men in pale robes scurrying about, mixing the contents of several containers.

"What're they doing?" She wanted to linger but Daniel urged her on with a maddening clucking sound made through

113

pursed lips.

"Conceiving." Then he added, "Don't you know anything?"

Penny blinked, studying Daniel to see if he was kidding, but the handsome face stared down at her, as serious as ever. "Dare I ask what they might be conceiving?"

Daniel snorted, showing what he thought of her ignorance. "Humans, of course."

This time Penny's mouth fell open. "Boy, you lot have made some changes since 1997."

Finally Daniel showed some curiosity to match Penny's. "Tell me about your life. You weren't very advanced in the Twentieth Century."

Purposefully Penny moved towards him. Brushing her breasts teasingly across his chest, she placed her hands on his impressive shoulders to draw him close. Unsurprisingly, he jumped back as though scorched.

"It is forbidden to touch a woman's breasts."

This was way out! "Don't men and women touch at all? Get together? *You know?*"

"Never."

You poor sods! "Surely a woman carries her child? I mean, once it's conceived in a petri dish? Or whatever you call them these days." The idea was so ridiculous that Penny fought to stifle a giggle.

"We have machines for that," Daniel announced proudly.

"Ah. Now, *that* development I can cheerfully go along with."

Daniel looked around nervously. "Come. I will take you to my home. The patrol will be out soon."

As they ambled along, Penny chatted. "Only one hundred years on, and you've made such drastic changes. It's difficult to assimilate. Hey! Just had a daunting thought," she joked, about to grab Daniel's arm when she thought better of it. "When I'm one hundred and twenty-five, I'll have to give up sex."

"*Before* you're one hundred and twenty-five. All this did

114

not happen overnight. Our society was created because too many human hours were being lost in the workforce. Absenteeism is nonexistent."

"You mean no one has a sickie? A day off," Penny elaborated when Daniel stared blankly at her. "God, I couldn't live without the odd sickie."

"There is no reason to remain at home. Men and women do not touch. Therefore there are no arguments. No –"

"How perfectly dull!" Penny retorted.

"On the contrary. We are allowed to read Twentieth Century history books. We will not make your mistakes by falling in love, allowing emotion to rule us. We do not have passion."

Wanna bet? Penny thought wickedly. Already Daniel was softening towards her. His vivid blue eyes were animated. And was that a sliver of excitement she could see?

Daniel's apartment was a revelation. In contrast to the sterile city, his private residence was bathed in bright colours and light. Heavily scented jonquils spilled from several vases placed around the room.

"This is more like it." Penny enthused, having expected the same dreariness that was outside. "I like a man who appreciates flowers."

Daniel, unable to feign disinterest a moment longer, bombarded her with questions. Penny, realising it was going to be a long night, flopped down into one of the sighing sofas and, tucking a leg beneath her, patted the spot next to her.

Thirty minutes later, Daniel was a changed man. The once stern features were softened, his blue eyes shone with an unbelievable brilliance, lips curved into a shy smile.

"I like the sound of your society. Tell me more."

Regaling him with tales of a sexy world, Penny snuggled closer. Daniel stroked her golden hair. "You smell beautiful."

"Would you like to kiss me, Daniel?"

He gazed thoughtfully into her dancing eyes. "Teach me."

Penny leaned over and kissed him lightly on the lips. After his initial surprise, he relaxed. Penny's lips began to caress the hard planes of his face, the softness of his eyes, the smooth yielding mouth. Momentarily, he tensed, then relaxed, his lips responding to hers. Her hand roved his chest, slipped down to his waist. Lower, to the slowly rising cock.

"Do you ever pleasure yourself?" Penny whispered, between flicking her tongue in and out of his ear. Any other man would be rock hard by now. "You know. Wank?"

"N-no," he gasped as Penny licked along his jaw, down his throat. "We … ah … we get monthly injections." Daniel squirmed, breathing harder at each dart of her tongue.

How weird! "So, you don't get erections? The urge?"

"No!" Daniel grabbed her breasts, as roughly as plucking two oranges from a tree.

Penny squealed. "Not like that! Gently. Like this." And her fingers searched out his own nipples, rotating them tenderly. "Run your tongue along my throat."

Tentatively, Daniel did as instructed, hesitating on the fringe of her breast. "May I?"

She watched his deep swallow as he awaited her reaction to his request.

Penny giggled, crossing her fingers as, blatantly, she lied. "You may boldly go where no man has gone before."

With gentle wonder he squeezed and stroked. Penny groaned, pushed Daniel away to draw her yellow top up and over her head. The wonder in Daniel's eyes took her breath away. When had a man last looked at her like that? As though she were God and Harry Potter rolled into one.

He drew a nipple into his mouth, began to suck. Penny threaded her fingers through his hair, held him close to her chest, groaning as Daniel suckled hard on her nipple, a thumb pressing on the other. *Sweet heaven! She was going to come already!* But she fought the urge. *Not yet.*

Then, pushing Daniel away, she ripped at his clothes, until he stood naked, his rod a fierce weapon pointing dangerously in the air.

"Oh, Christ! Yes! Come here, baby."

She gripped his cock, let her fingers dance up and down its

length. Down to his balls, grazing with her nails, until he gasped with pleasure. There was a tiny bead of moisture on the tip, and Penny sucked it into her mouth. Daniel shuddered. And this was only a foretaste of what was to come! She flattened one hand against his abdomen and felt taut, strong muscles beneath it. Her mouth encircled his cock.

He jerked away. Then hastily pushed his rod back into her face, so she was sheathing him once more. "What! I don't ... don't ... yes! Please!" And Penny's tongue swirled the head of his shaft.

In response, her A-plus student slid his hand up under Penny's muslin skirt, along her bare legs. His fingers burrowed beneath her panties. Sighing with pleasure when he touched the silky skin at her centre, Penny opened her legs. He played with the soft folds, discovered the small bead, caressed it lovingly.

"Show me how to interlock with you." Daniel's voice was husky, and there were sweat beads on his forehead.

Penny spluttered. "I've heard it called some crazy names before but ..." She grinned. "Come here my little Lego-piece!"

Her thighs fell open, giving a good view of what was to come. Then, touching his cock and drawing him near, Penny remembered she was his first woman. How utterly erotic was that? As the tip of him connected with her velvety place, she shivered in anticipation, and the shudder that went through Daniel delighted her.

There was much more to show him; she would have loved more foreplay, but it was obvious that he couldn't wait to experience the main course. After instructing her lover to pick her up she wrapped her legs round his waist. "Now, lower me down onto your cock. That's right. All the way. Ah," Penny sighed when he filled her. "Now push up into my cunt. Higher! Harder!" Catching the rhythm, thrusting his cock deep inside her, his pubic bone rubbing her clitoris, Penny squealed. "Ah. That ... that's right. Keep going. Grind ... hard. Fuck me! Come on, fuck me!"

117

She screamed.

Daniel thought he was fucking her. Her words added to his excitement; sent little shivers along his spine. And his cock throbbed like he didn't think was possible. It was both a part of him, yet an entity all its own. "Oh, my God! I … I feel like … erupting."

"No, no. Not yet!" But it was too late; he squirted into her. On and on, as if he had been saving it all for her. With his body giving a long, violent shudder, she held him close until he was spent.

Shortly afterwards, Daniel wanted more, his hands roving over her. Fingers in her cunt, lips on her tits.

"Greedy, aren't you?" Penny smiled, and the naked lust in his eyes sprinkled warm tingles through her body. Already his shaft was engorged, pressing urgently into her flesh. She decided to show him what she liked most; then it would be Daniel's turn and she knew already he was crazy for it.

As Daniel watched, Penny got on the floor, reclining, opening her legs under his attentive fascination. "Come here, lover boy," she coaxed.

When he knelt between her thighs she instructed him to put his face right up to her pussy. "Now. Lick me." He soon got the hang of it and Penny lost herself in the sensation, sighing with pleasure. Before long he was improvising. Using lots of saliva, lapping between her sex lips, while his hands caressed her inner thighs. With gentle teeth he took her clit into his mouth, sucking strongly while she groaned and squirmed in his face. Soon his tongue was playing along her slit, pressing hard when he reached the bud, licking round it with expert manipulation. Making circles round her clit with the tip of his tongue.

On the verge of climax, Penny held Daniel's head so that the entire pressure was on her tiny shaft. "Aaaah. More! More!" Within seconds she came, long and loud and intense. The sweetest orgasm of her life! Finally, her body relaxed and through half-opened eyes she gazed at Daniel. Obviously very proud of his achievement, he was smiling.

"That was nice. You taste … nice. I don't know. It's difficult to define. Oh, Penny! Since you walked into my century my existence is full of pleasure. My skin zings with anticipation. Do women lick men like that? You know. Until they come? I really want you to lick me like a … a lollipop!" He beamed, proud of his simile.

"Oh, so you know what a lollipop is, then, do you?" Penny looked around for something to use as a blindfold. Her discarded top would do. With his puzzled gaze upon her Penny explained that this would heighten sensations, and tied the fabric over his eyes.

Reaching out, she asked him to stand while she got to her knees, coming up close to the jutting penis. "This is what you are supposed to do before you begin licking a woman. Don't go straight for the cunt. Play a little. Tease her."

If Daniel wondered why she was telling him this now, after the event, he forgot all about it as she stood, and began licking from his shoulder, to his chest, sucking his small tits into her mouth. Air sucked loudly through his teeth as his body shuddered. A*h, he liked that, did, he?* When she was ready, she licked down his body, ever closer to the throbbing cock. Daniel was becoming agitated, grunting, groaning. Rocking back and forth so his rod was pressing into her.

"Patience, my lovely."

Many times she took him to the brink of orgasm. Long slides up and down his rigid length, taking him in her mouth, coating him with saliva. He bucked like a bronco, until she cupped his balls and gently fingered them, rotating the hard marble she felt inside. His smell was musky, yet sweet, the aroma of sex swirling round her. Daniel was her love slave. She felt she could do anything, ask anything. She pressed her finger between the stem of his cock and his anus until he shuddered. Taking him to another level, she anointed one finger inside her slit, then slipped it gently, slowly, deep inside him. Almost immediately his cock began to jerk, spasm in her mouth and Daniel thrust harder, harder, as he came. She withdrew as he ejaculated, and with a shout of triumph

119

observed the contortions on his face, the animal grunts he made as semen spouted upwards, then down.

By the early hours of the morning Daniel and Penny were exhausted. A sweetly intoxicating aroma mingled with perspiration emanating from their entwined bodies. They fell asleep, Daniel's smile a reflection of Penny's.

Something soft and exciting was weaving damp patches across her skin.

"I like the soft flesh of a woman," Daniel murmured, his kisses becoming more urgent now that Penny was awake. "I like your 1997."

Penny hadn't given thought to getting back to her own time but now, with Daniel's reminder, she sailed from the bed, quickly pulling on her clothes.

"I'll need to find a rainbow to travel home, I guess." Otherwise how was she to get back? As wonderful as Daniel was, she wanted to go home. Behind closed doors it was great, but outside, 2097 appeared a scary place.

"There is one scheduled at noon today."

Penny smiled. "You continue to amaze me."

She rushed for the bathroom and out, then lingered a moment to gaze at this lovely man's gorgeous face, when he said, "I'm coming with you, Penny."

Throwing her arms around him, she squealed. "Really? Come on then, but hurry."

Daniel needed no further bidding. Without thought she had accepted his intention.

Panting from their sprint across town, Penny rested her palms on her shaky knees and inhaled lungfuls of air. When she straightened she voiced the alarming thought that suddenly materialized. "My sister was with me," she gulped. "But I was the only one transported."

Daniel's analytical mind went to work. "Were you touching?"

She shook her head.

Her lover's lazy smile sent shivers of desire cascading

through Penny.

"We will have to interlock. If our bodies are joined, the beam will transport us as one."

Walking hand in hand to the foot of the rainbow, Daniel smiled. Then he lifted her. Instinctively Penny's legs encircled his waist, heels digging into his firm buttocks, urging him closer.

Gratified at the hardness of his penis, Penny demanded, "Put your cock inside me. Now!"

Waiting for the spectrum to lift them, with Penny squirming provocatively, her pussy clutching him tightly, Daniel rested his chin on sweet Penny's hair and murmured, "What a way to travel."

Whack!
by Ivana Chopski

The room was quiet now apart from the incessant tick, tick, tick of the alarm clock on the bedside table. Brian wanted desperately to turn his head and see how long he'd been lying there; he didn't though as that wasn't part of the deal.

He was home from work first today and he'd desperately wanted to hunt through her wardrobe and find out what she was hiding in there before she got in. He knew she was hiding something but if he looked and found it, whatever 'it' was, he would spoil the surprise. And the surprise was the most important thing after all. The anticipation, the thrill of the unknown, it turned him on. It turned him on a lot. He was getting hard just thinking about it but he didn't have time for that now; he needed to be ready before she got home.

He was in the bath when Amanda came home from work just as they planned. She'd come upstairs with a bottle of Chardonnay and two glasses, then sat on the toilet as they shared the wine and chatted about the day. They both behaved as if this wasn't premeditated, trying to keep a calm exterior while the excitement raged on inside. Amanda toyed with him by slipping down her knickers and having a wee on the toilet and as he pretended not to watch she exaggerated her movements as she wiped herself with a piece of toilet tissue. She could see a bit of movement under the bubbles and smiled to herself, Brian said nothing. He was feeling quite light-headed as he got out of the bath, a combination of the warm water and a half a bottle of wine and he was happy to let Amanda towel him down. He wasn't as dry as he would have

123

liked but still took her hand as she led him across the hall into the bedroom.

Amanda let go of his hand and he stood naked next to the bed as he watched her puff up the pillows then part them slightly, leaving a small gap between them. She hadn't changed out of her work clothes and her suit skirt clung tightly to her backside as she bent over the bed, Brian looked at her longingly and his cock started to stiffen. Amanda noticed the rise in blood pressure as she turned round, smiling to herself and as she walked past him 'accidentally' brushed her hand along his penis. Brian heard himself gasp then coloured up slightly as if he had betrayed himself, Amanda appeared not to hear. She stopped at the dressing table by the window and opened the third drawer on the right at the same time beckoning Brian onto the bed. His mouth had gone dry.

He lay face down on the bed with his face tucked in between the recently puffed pillows then pointed his arms and legs towards each corner of the bed. He was unable to see that she had taken four large silk scarves out of the drawer but he had known that was what she'd done. Brian heard her pad towards the bed in her stockinged feet then hitch up her skirt so she could straddle his back. His cock started to throb, constrained as it was, squashed against his stomach. It was squashed even further as Amanda sat on the small of his back. She started to move herself slowly up his back, he could feel the soft silk of her panties and through the flimsy material her hot moist pussy, she stopped when she got to his shoulders and took hold of his right arm.

Amanda chose one of the scarves and expertly tied one end around Brian's wrist and the other to the bedstead. When she was happy with the knots she did the same to his left wrist then turned around moved down to his legs. Amanda repeated the process, attaching a scarf to each ankle then in turn to the footboard; Brian was convinced that he could free himself from the scarves if he wanted to, though he had never tried. Amanda knew he couldn't.

She got off the bed now and walked out of the room

without saying a word and walked downstairs, Brian strained with all his might to hear what she was up to. He could hear nothing and started to relax slightly, all of him that is apart from his raging hard-on. He heard her mount the stairs and he tensed up again, unsure of what to expect – Amanda never did the same thing twice. She walked back into the bedroom with two aromatherapy tea-light candles, one she placed on the bedside table and the other on the wardrobe and lit them both. He could smell the fragrance, one was lavender, he was sure but couldn't place the other one, he didn't linger too long on the scent as he turned his mind to what Amanda was up to. He heard her open her wardrobe and he held his breath, was she opening it to take something out or to put her clothes away? He started to breathe again as he heard a hanger rattle and presumed the latter.

Brian was right; Amanda stepped out of her skirt and hung up her suit for another day, rolled down her hold-ups then took off her blouse and bra, all of which she tossed into the laundry basket. She stood at the end of the bed in her tiny thong and looked at Brian. He heard her get on the bed between his legs before he felt her breath on the inside of his calves, the gentle warm breath was moving slowly upwards. Brian's hard-on was raging again and ready to explode as she took one of his balls in her mouth shortly followed by the other. She managed to alternate between rolling them around her mouth and sucking on them until Brian was about to reach a climax, Amanda anticipated this and to stop him she opened her mouth, letting his balls flop onto the bed as she stood up.

Brian heard her shuffling next to the bed; he couldn't work out what she was doing – then he felt silky soft material on his back. As she walked up the bed she ran the material up his spine and dropped it on the pillow next to his face as she turned out the light and left the room. He didn't need to look to know that it was her knickers, inches from his face, because he could smell the sweet musky odour of her sex, he grinned to himself because now he knew she was feeling as horny as he was.

He could hear her starting to run herself a bath; he tried to make himself comfortable as he was sure he was going to be there some time. The ambiance in the room, with the gentle glow of the candles, as well as the half bottle of wine he had recently consumed was helping him to relax but he didn't want to relax too much in case she caught him off-guard. He forced himself to listen to what she was doing in case she was using the noise of the running water to sneak back into the bedroom. He couldn't hear her at all.

He could feel his knob throbbing again and was not sure why, although it was always like this. Was it the anticipation or the helplessness? he thought to himself, or the fear of the unknown? Maybe it was the pain; sometimes she hurt him, not in a bad way but a good way. How the fuck did that make any sense, how could you be hurt in a good way? It did make sense though; if someone punched him in the face that was a bad hurt but when Amanda squeezed his balls tightly or pinched his nipples that was a good hurt. He wasn't sure what it was; maybe it was a combination of all four, whatever it was it made him as horny as fuck, and what about Amanda? Where did she get her kicks from all of this? and she definitely did get a kick out of it because it made her fucking rampant. Brian hoped she didn't get off on hurting him; he was sure she didn't, he'd never asked her just in case but presumed she loved the whole package like him.

He heard her get into the bath; he felt he could relax for a little while and listened to her bathing. He imagined her lying back in the bath, resting her head on that little pink inflatable pillow he had bought her and splashing the water on her chest. He closed his eyes and could see a droplet of warm water run down from her neck and onto her large pearly white breast; he tracked its path with his finger. The water ran downwards stopping for a moment on her nipple and his finger traced its outline until gravity encouraged the droplet further south and his finger followed. Followed until it reached the neatly trimmed bush that hid the droplet of water from view in a river of hidden treasure.

Brian licked his lips as he thought about running his finger around the outline of her hairy axe wound. She always pulled a face when he called it that, as if she was outraged, but he really knew that was for show and she was smiling on the inside. He was thinking so hard about it he thought he could almost smell it then realized that her panties were still inches from his face and he probably could, this made him chuckle to himself. Scratch and sniff he thought! In his mind his finger was working its way through the hair to find her pussy lips which he gently caressed for a few moments until he forced his way in between and began to massage her clitoris. He could feel it grow and harden to his touch and could imagine it throb like his aching cock. He moved slightly to make himself more comfortable and heard her groan; the noise was for real he realized, not coming from the depths of his imagination. The horny bitch was pleasuring herself in the bath while he was tied to the fucking bed nursing the hard-on of all hard-ons.

How did that make him feel? He wasn't sure about that either. She must know that he could hear her and was making no attempt to disguise it so it must be all part of her plan and whatever she was trying to achieve, something was definitely affected. If she didn't get out of that bath soon he was going to fucking explode. He moved his arms slightly to see if he could escape from the bed and the knots seemed to tighten with the slightest movement. Then the moaning stopped and he heard a bit of splashing, the plug pulled from the hole and Amanda getting out of the bath. He was so ready for it now he could feel himself coming out in a cold sweat, his heart was racing, the hairs on his neck stood on end and his cock felt like it was on fire. Still she made him wait.

She dried herself slowly with the large towel she took off the radiator then wrapped it around herself as she stood in front of the bathroom mirror and spent a couple of minutes on her hair. Then she went across to the shelf by the window and looked at her collection of perfumes, picked up a couple and put them back before she chose the most suitable one for tonight. Brian smelt the perfume before she entered the room,

127

it was new and he liked it, now it was moving away from him. His body tingled with anticipation as he heard the wardrobe open, this time she was getting something out.

Amanda hid it behind her back, unsure why as his face was burrowed in the pillows, just in case maybe he turned around and spoilt the surprise? She stood by the side of the bed and waited; she wanted to do it now but knew the wait would fuck with his senses. When she was so hot she could wait no more she brought it out from behind her back, raised it above her head then: WHACK!

Office Crush
by Sadie Wolf

I once spent a year in Australia, working nine to five in an office ten minutes' walk from the famous harbour. At lunchtime I often sat and ate my sandwiches on a bench with views of the bridge and the opera house. Tourists would stop and ask me to take their photographs, and their happiness was infectious. It was like stepping right into a picture postcard, but amazing as it was, it wasn't the scenery that made the strongest impression on me.

The office I worked in was essentially open-plan, with screens dividing it up into smaller areas where teams of four or so people worked. A handful of more senior staff had offices with proper walls and doors off the main area, but with plenty of glass so that they weren't particularly private. One of these offices was right by my area, and I had to pass its door, which was invariably open, every time I left or returned to my desk. I felt an initial awkwardness about its inhabitants – Monique, a senior caseworker, and Mathew, the manager of another team. I wondered if I should smile or say hello every time I passed, which would have been ridiculous, or not to bother, which might look standoffish? I needn't have worried. Monique was almost always ensconced behind her desk in the far corner, busy typing or on the phone; and Mathew … well, he simply failed to acknowledge my existence.

He didn't immediately strike me as especially good looking. He was mid- to late-thirties with close-cropped hair, and a serious, unfriendly expression permanently on his face. He was one of only two other English people in the office, but if I had expected this to create a bond between us, I would have been wrong. He was from Manchester, and spoke in a flat Mancunian drawl that only served to accentuate his grumpy persona. He'd emigrated fifteen years ago and had never been back. You had to be tough to do that, or it made you tough. I was homesick enough just being away for a year.

He never actually spoke to me, although I often heard him having quite animated conversations with other people, often people I was on quite friendly terms with. Sometimes I would finish a conversation with someone and return to my desk, and a few minutes later hear Mathew talking to that same person in his office. I tried to imagine them acting as some kind of bridge between Mathew and me, making some kind of connection between us. I suppose the fact that he ignored me only made me more interested. I sneaked glances at him when he was sitting at his desk, and was acutely aware of when he was passing my work area. I noticed his face and arms were tanned, and that his body was lean and well-muscled; apparently he did a lot of running.

I started making more effort with my appearance in the mornings. People commented on my hair, my clothes. I found myself increasingly conscious of my body, my movements. When I walked past his office, I was acutely aware of my walk, my steps, like walking in and out of time to a beat I wasn't familiar with.

I considered myself fortunate to have a desk by a window, and I often found myself gazing out of it, daydreaming. There was a busy junction right outside, and I often winced while observing the frequent near misses involving motorists and pedestrians.

I used to daydream about getting hit by a car just as Mathew was coming back from the coffee shop, and him picking me up and taking me to the hospital, and me lying in his arms looking pale and vulnerable, and a special bond being created between us. Him visiting me at the hospital and us eating grapes and talking, and him realising what an interesting person I am, and me realising he only seems cold

130

because he hasn't met the right woman yet … Or even if I just got hit by a car and turned up to work with a full leg plaster and crutches. He would definitely look at me then, maybe even comment, and would surely help me up if I fell down in front of him. But would he all of a sudden notice my eyes, my tits? I began to worry about being invisible.

In August it was my birthday, and I brought in cakes for the office. After lunch I found myself alone with him in the kitchen. I took a deep breath.

'There's some cake over there if you want some.'

'What's the occasion?' He picked up his cup of coffee.

'It's my birthday.'

'Twenty-one again?' He opened the door. I tried desperately to think of something to say, but by the time I had opened my mouth, he'd shut the door behind him. I stood there alone, hugging my stomach, which was turning over and over, feeling foolish and excited all at the same time.

I had two friends in the office, who I sometimes went out for coffee with and who between them helped me to survive the office. Lucy was sharp, blonde and pretty. She entertained us with boyfriend stories. Sam was English and had a little girl, and was strong and warm-hearted. When we gossiped about people in the office, Mathew's name would come up periodically. We all agreed that there was something seriously wrong with him, the way he was so anti-social, never talked to us and always looked so moody. *And* he was lazy, always reading the paper at his desk when he should have been working. Although inevitably one of us would start giggling, and we would grudgingly admit that yes, he was horrible, but he was also – horror of horrors – actually quite fit. Although not that any of us would actually … of course not, no way! According to Lucy he was dating some woman who had wooed him by cooking him fancy Russian dinners. We all agreed that she sounded pretentious and that, in any case, she must be mad, poor woman, to go out with him.

The office was divided up into teams, with each team managing its own list of clients. In addition to this everyone in the office took turns to hold the duty phone, dealing with miscellaneous queries that the reception staff couldn't answer, or handling urgent problems when the caseworker responsible was unavailable.

Now, I was competent at my job. I was conscientious and looked after my clients well. I didn't like holding the duty phone though, because you never knew what was coming, and you could be faced with having to sort out all sorts of problems without knowing anything about the background. One particular afternoon when I had the phone, everything had been pretty quiet, only ringing with everyday queries I could easily deal with. Then a call came through from one of Mathew's clients. Mathew was out of the office and couldn't be contacted. His client was calling from a hotel in Bangkok, in a furious panic because a vital piece of paperwork was missing. I did my best to reassure him, took down the phone and fax numbers of the hotel and got to work in the file room. I found his file easily enough, but it was in such a mess that it took me some time to find what I was looking for.

I prayed that the fax machine wouldn't choose this moment to play up – luckily it didn't – then rang him back to tell him what I had done.

He sounded too relieved to be annoyed any more, and I felt as if I had just headed off a potential disaster. Mathew was due back in the office at four, and I was so irrationally excited about his return that I forgot to be nervous about holding the phone.

He arrived back in the office and began talking to Monique. I waited a couple of minutes, then I picked up his client's file and the phone, and knocked tentatively on the open door.

'Hi Julie.' Monique was friendly enough, as always.

'What can we do for you?' Mathew drawled, looking at me for what felt like the first time. My mission gave me a purpose, and some confidence. I stepped into the office and sat down on a chair opposite Mathew's desk. *I'm sitting in his office.*

'I had a call on the duty phone from one of your clients –
Mr Mason, in Bangkok?'

His face registered this information. He laughed.

'Oh shit. I bet he was after that spreadsheet?'

'That's the one. I faxed it to his hotel, it's all OK now.'

He leaned back in his chair. I tried not to stare at his
forearms, bare below his rolled up shirtsleeves.

'Knew I'd forgotten something. Well, thanks for that. You
can just put that file back for me.'

'No problem.'

He turned back to Monique. *Say something.*

'Lucky him, must be exciting, jetting off to Bangkok.'

'Horrible place. Far too hot, full of traffic fumes.'

He looked at me. My stomach contracted. Was he *smirking*
at me?

'Right, well, I guess I'd better -.' I picked up the phone and
waved it vaguely.

'Has it been busy, Julie?' Monique asked kindly.

'Er, no, not really ...' I trailed off. Mathew appeared
absorbed in his paperwork. I stood up.

'OK ... bye.' I don't think he even bothered saying
goodbye.

I had been assigned a small research project to do, but between
looking after my clients and the distractions of a busy office I
was beginning to despair of ever getting it completed. I knew
my boss often came in on a Sunday to catch up on paperwork,
so I asked him if I could do the same. He said I was welcome
to, and that he and his wife were flying to Melbourne for the
weekend so I would probably have the office to myself.

When the alarm went off on Sunday morning, I resisted the
temptation to switch it off and go back to sleep. The sun was
coming in through the curtains, and although the bed was
lovely and warm, getting up didn't seem such a bad idea. I
stretched and hugged myself awake, then rolled out of bed and
wandered naked straight into the shower. The hot water felt
good, made me feel awake and energised. I washed and

conditioned my hair, shaved my legs, and after I had towelled myself dry I put on body lotion and perfume and painted my nails. It felt good to pull on jeans for going into work. I put on a thin black cashmere jumper without a bra, to enjoy the feeling of it against my skin.

I blow-dried my hair and put on a little make-up, then picked up my bag and headed out the door, humming a little tune to myself. I felt light and free, and proud of myself for getting up early.

The change in routine gave me a lift, and I thought about how silly I was, to feel so excited about going into work on a Sunday.

I opened the main door using my passkey. The boss was right – there didn't seem to be anyone else around. I opened the door to the file room, putting out my hand to feel for the light switch as I stepped inside. Before I found it, I screamed – I had touched someone. The someone grabbed hold of my wrist, really hard, and I looked up and saw Mathew. Fear turned to relief, and back to fear. A jolt of electricity shot through my belly, and our eyes locked.

'I'm sorry.' He let go of me. He put the light on and I sat down on the table. I could feel myself trembling. This was the closest we had ever been to each other.

'I'm sorry.' I said, even though I didn't know why I was apologising.

'Nervous aren't you? I was just switching off the light when I heard a noise. I wasn't expecting anyone else to come in today. Sorry. Did I hurt your wrist?'

I held out my arm. My wrist had a red mark around it. He picked it up, lightly, casually, as if he was picking up a pencil, or a piece of paper, and kissed it on the red mark.

'Cold are you? Good job it's Sunday, you'd drive your clients wild.' He was staring unashamedly at my chest, an amused expression on his face. My nipples were hard and quite noticeable through the thin cashmere.

Then, casually, as if he was doing nothing at all out of the ordinary, he took hold of the hem of my sweater and pulled it

134

off over my head. He knelt down and kissed my nipples, taking them in his mouth. It felt delicious, but after a few seconds, he stopped.

'If anyone came here, I'd get all the blame, and you could say it was sexual harassment, even though you've been making eyes at me for months.'

'No. I wouldn't do that.'

'Prove it.' He looked down at the floor in front of his feet, and I understood. I knelt down on the floor in front of him. He undid his belt, and the zip of his trousers. The smell of him was like a drug ... all soapy sweetness. I reached into his trousers, pulling down his black cotton shorts and exposing his cock, which was thick and hard, and quivering slightly, right in front of my face. I felt a ringing in my ears as I closed my eyes and took him into my mouth. I put my hands on his thighs, feeling a thrill of pride that they were shaking slightly. *So, there is a way to get to him.*

I concentrated as hard as I could on the task in hand, licking the length of his cock to make it slippery and easy to take in, and taking it as far back as I could. I let my hands explore his thighs and his balls, which were hard and felt full to bursting. When he came, he held the back of my head with his hands and thrust into me, fucking my mouth.

I spent the next three months being his whore. No one was supposed to know. He had forbidden me from telling anyone at all. Monique once raised an eyebrow at me, giving me a funny look, and I blushed and felt embarrassed, but she never said anything. I never went to his house, nor he to mine. Little pieces of paper would appear in my pigeonhole: *8pm Wednesday* and I'd cancel whatever I was doing and be there. We always did it at work, in the file room, because at least that had a lock. He never took me on a date, or even so much as bought me a drink.

Most of the time he didn't even fuck me, much less caress or cuddle me. Our encounters were clinical, emotionally cold, yet he left me desperate for more, absolutely in thrall to him and his wishes.

I never found out why he stopped. Maybe he was worried about people finding out, or maybe he had decided to settle down properly with the Russian cookery expert, I don't know. I was devastated at the time, of course, but there was nothing I could do. It wasn't as if we even talked about it – talking wasn't something we ever did. But I tried to keep my chin up, and one of the things that helped was remembering our last time. It felt so special that even now I feel sure he must have planned it specially, in order to do me a final kindness.

He'd left me a little note, as usual, except that this time it was handwritten instead of typed, and actually had a little kiss at the bottom. After he had locked the door of the file room behind us, he actually sat down on the floor next to me and talked to me for a little while. Not about anything earth-shattering, just a little small talk about work and the office, but it meant a lot. It made it feel a bit more normal, less degrading, than his usual practice of just undoing his trousers. I knew something was up when he kissed me before doing anything else, then lay me down on the floor and held me, chest against chest, so that I could feel his heart beating.

I love you, I love you, I love you. I had to bite my tongue to stop the words escaping, but the feelings spilt out anyway, tears falling down my face as he made love to me. He let go of me and pulled me onto his lap, so that I was sitting on him, his arms around my waist. All I wanted was to hide in his chest, but he made me sit up straight and look at him. He stared right at me, watching my tits as I moved slowly on top of him.

'You're beautiful, you've got great tits.' I held on tight to these words that he had never said before. I knew it would be all too easy to think later that I had imagined them. He hooked his fingers around the base of my back, pulling me up, down, forward, back, until black spots started to appear in front of my eyes and it was all I could do to follow his rhythm. I felt as though I were dissolving, as if the edges of my body and his had blurred, leaving only the interface where we were touching and burning, melting and dissolving together. I couldn't believe, at that moment, that he didn't love me too; maybe not in the way I loved him, but somehow, in his own way. It just didn't seem possible that something could feel so much like love, if really it was nothing at all.

Afterwards I fell onto his chest and he put his arms around me and stroked my hair and I felt so *grateful. Thank you, thank you, thank you.* I think I knew then that it was over, but I didn't want to listen to the voice of reason in my head. Instead, I said to myself, here is the man for me, I have finally met my match. This is the man I would renounce my country for, my family. As if saying it in my head would somehow make it all come true.

Alley Kat
by Alcamia

My name is Katrina and I always look impeccable in my starched white blouse and sensible shoes. However, I am far from little miss purity. I have a very dirty secret. Whenever I step into an alley, I shed my innocent Katrina skin and I become filthy alley Kat.

Dirty Tom cat, has been following the essence of my pussy for weeks. He has teased and sniffed around the fringes of my sexuality until I am simmering with lust. Now, tonight, like any predator stalking his prey, he has entered attack mode and I am sharpening my kitty claws ready for his advances. Tonight is my initiation. You see, to be fucked up Alley Zero, is like a right of passage, through which I have to pass to awaken my new found sexual liberation. I have been trapped in a dry wasteland of 'no sex' for far too long. In fact I have been in a state of alley virginity for as long as I can remember, because it is not easy to find a dirty Tom who can fulfil your filthiest fantasy

Tom cat is following me out of the club. He is stalking the essence of my tantalising pussy musk. I draw into the shadows, licking my lips at the prospect of the meal to come and my amber eyes dilate in anticipation.

I am liquescent. So turned on I am breathless. He really lit my fuse when he danced with me earlier. Smothering my mouth, grinding his hips into my quim. From that moment, he marked his territory on me and I had no desire to escape his claws. I simply began to purr.

I sniff and lick at the feral scent of alley Tom cat on my

hands, and its filthy key note explodes within my neural synapses, sending a surge of excitement though my body.

Where are you, Tom cat? I know you are somewhere in the shadows, toying with me like a cat toys with a mouse. My body stiffens with sex impulse. My cunt is sopping wet. The moist sex juice, is like rainfall on a dry desert. It makes my pussy seed germinate, erupt and blossom, and I quiver with orgasmic ripples.

I exude sex appeal. It oozes out of my feline pores. Men pursue me because they smell alley Kat all over my hot body and they just love that wild pussy odour. They sniff at the dirty undertones and instantly they are spellbound by my alley cat vibe. They adore my slinky sexuality, purring vibrato voice, long claws and savage, wild cat eyes. Most of all they love the smell of alley Kat sex honey, oozing from my cunt. Naturally, I fight them all off. Only one kind of mate appeals to this kitty, and that is one as down and dirty as me. Mr Tom cat.

I feel the familiar glow of expectant sex and my internal sexual barometer begins to rise, as he steps out of the shadows. He is just the kind of cat I adore. Rough and territorial with emerald, deep set eyes and a dangerous twist to sardonic lips. The moment I laid eyes on him, I knew he had grown out of the filth and graffiti. He was a true urban child of the alley.

A jolt of electricity stiffens my nipples. Tom cat creeps up on me and holds me captive. His voracious tongue probing my mouth. He can feel the fire rising through my skin, as he presses against my writhing body and my pulse escalates, giving birth to the flowing juices which stain my thighs. Tom cat makes me flow like a geyser and the pussy cat cream just keeps coming and coming.

He continues to kiss me with rapier stabbing motions of his darting tongue. This is not the gentle kiss of a lover, but the hungry desire of a copulation seeking animal. Insistently the tongue keeps working the inside of my mouth, igniting my circuit of eroticism. Sending arousing stimuli through my sexual network. It triggers nipple and clit, and soft welcoming pussy. He presses me up against the damp bricks of the alley and his hips grind me into the viscous, semen-painted walls. Then, lips and tongue chase the blue vein, down my bare arm, as if he is pursuing the essence of pussy cat through my blood. I sink my nails into his skin and my purr intensifies. I fire again and again, in rapid convulsions, his hands kneading my buttocks, first one then the other. Sliding my skirt up to caress my thighs, he probes between my legs, rubbing my liquid crease through my flimsy panties. I run my tongue over my lips in further invitation.

'I have this obsession with getting fucked up an alley. Actually, it's the only place I can fuck.' I moan, low and vibrato.

'I'm going to eat and then fuck you.' He says huskily. 'I'm going to lap at that kitty cat milk, and I'm going to suck the cream.'

Excitement sends shots of adrenaline through my system and my plump white breasts swell and recede beneath my tight corset. I grip the hard bulge in his pants with my strong fist and I knead him with my paws, pulling him closer as I slide my arms around his tight butt. Tom cat's lean hips will feel so good, pumping my drought-dry pussy. I can hardly contain myself. My addiction has not been fed for months, and like any addict, I desire my fix.

I don't know what made me like this. Perhaps it is in my genes, or maybe it is because the first thing I ever laid eyes on was the alley, and they say you have a definitive tie to your birthplace. You see, my mother gave birth to me in an alleyway. She rarely talked about it, after all that was her dirty secret. But as a result I think I am a little tainted by the down and dirty vibe, of the pussy cat hunting ground.

When the pain took her, my mother was surprised as she had not made much of an effort to ascertain her due date and I literally dropped into her life like a bombshell. I was born in the alley as she could not walk any further and she had needed to crawl into secrecy to have me. She birthed me like a kitten, quickly and in the dark shadow of a fire escape. Apparently, I was easy in my arrival but I squealed like a banshee. Later, as a child I sought out the darkness of passageways. The memory of filthy dark places was instilled in me and appealed to my sense of urban mystery. My mother was a whore and men came and went at all hours of the day and night from our Islington flat. My mother's behaviour got up my nose to such an extent, I walked the streets like an orphan, detesting the return to the flat which always reeked of cheap booze, stale perfume and sex. Or I would sit surrounded by mewling cats in the alley, my true home. Of course, my mother threatened me with punitive measures if I kept returning there, but I didn't take any notice. It was my happy hunting ground, and what did she care anyway. All my mother was concerned about was her next bottle of gin or new pair of shoes.

I was always slightly strange Katrina, but I can remember the day I changed my name to alley Kat and discovered the licentious depths to which I had evidently sunk. I was staying with Marvine in New York before I started university.

Marvine and I had been to a burger joint to see her boyfriend, Jerome. I could tell instantly that he had a thing about me. I had met him several times by then, and his eyes always probed lasciviously beneath my clothes, seeking the bud of firm nipple and the contours of juicy sex. I possessed the feral stink of alley cat, and he was drawn to me, and saw something in me which was kinky and arousing. The three of us walked out from the burger joint together, straight into a noisy parade, there always seemed to be one in New York. I became separated from Marvine and I panicked a little.

Darting inside an opening, I found myself in the mouth of an alley. Marvine had underlined that I was not to take short cuts. But in the daylight it seemed harmless enough and, I deduced from my calculations, it must exit somewhere near Marvine's apartment. Jerome was behind me and that gave me a curious sexual thrill. I felt no sense of alarm, simply the familiar moistening of kitty milk, between my legs. I knew he wanted to fuck me, but until now, he could not find a way to get me alone. The anonymity of the dark alleyway fuelled my desire and I flexed my claws. I was thrumming with lust as pressing against me, he began to fondle my breasts and taking my hand he placed it on his monster cock. I tugged at his zipper, having great difficultly getting it to move over his mammoth erection. Jerome hitched up my skirt and, ripping down my thong, he began to fuck me with the ferocious abandon of a feral alley cat.

When I returned to England, I became a student in that most poetic of cities: Cambridge. I would walk within the university alleyways, absorbing the ancient bodies and ancient sex. On occasion, a student would accost me and I would allow him to. No one was immune to my kitty magic. Sometimes the accosting was of a mild nature. A sharing of hand and tongue. At other times it was ferocious, primal copulation.

As I developed in alley sexuality, I found they brought out my most indecent behaviour. Within them, I became a performer stepping onto a stage, and I metamorphosed out of my clean Katrina skin, and into dirty Kat. Here, I could act out my darkest desires and be whoever I wanted to be. I never tried to analyse it. I just accepted the fact I was born of the alley.

There is no getting away from it, sex happens in alleys and alleys have a certain sex appeal which makes my juices flow. I hide in the shadows to witness men unzipping their trousers and masturbating. Sex starved teenagers, thirsty lesbians unable to wait. The best performance of all was the sex of a well dressed couple coming home from the theatre, the woman exquisite in her low cut designer gown. Obscene in their grunting and coupling, it was the mating dance par excellence of two octopuses. They were all arms and legs, tangling and rippling. He spread her on the wall, lifted her taffeta froth of skirt and, like a battering ram, he took her. I was so turned on, I simply couldn't help rubbing furiously at my clit and I came with such an explosion I gave a small cry and the couple froze. That was certainly a close call. From that day on, the salacious alley was an unquenchable magnet and I returned as often as I could to investigate its activities.

I acquired a working knowledge of every alley in my neighbourhood. I made it my mission to be the foremost authority. I'd study the minutiae of their physiology like a scientist examining a particularly interesting microbe under a microscope. Like a human organism they possessed body, breath and heart and certain idiosyncrasies all of their own. I sorted through trash cans and I found items to both titillate and amuse. Sexual life stories were thrown away in the trash. Once my finger rested on a spot of milky semen and that really fired me up. This sex was new, perhaps only minutes old. Ancient semen and daring thoughts only served to arouse me more, and I would sink down onto my haunches and slide my fingers into my lubricious fanny, orgasming almost instantaneously.

Which leads me on to the source of my most prolific finds. Alley Zero. The alley, par excellence! It is my alley cat hunting ground and the place I choose for my latest initiation. Entering Alley Zero from the club is like finding the back of the wardrobe in the 'Narnia Chronicles'. It permits entry for the select few into alley heaven. Alley Zero hums with a filthy energy all of its own and it is such a fertile hunting ground, there is no alley quite like it in the whole of my city. In Alley Zero I discovered condoms so large they must have fitted monster cocks; Discarded knickers and thongs; dirty books, pornographic pictures, a mistress's whip and Oh yes; electrical items with and without the batteries. My most erotic find was an artificial vagina lurking in the bottom of a dustbin. The moist, gaping pussy, really attracted my attention and I plunged my fingers into it, working them around to get a feel for the artificial maw, and how it might seem to a man's cock. It now takes up pride of place on my mantelpiece amongst my other alley trophies. You could call me a collector par excellence of alley memorabilia.

I think some hooker lives in an apartment overlooking Alley Zero. After all, no ordinary person would possess so many gadgets. Now, my primary objective is to be fucked there. Fucked in the most thorough way. While under the

144

watchful eye of the invisible hooker.

'I know what you want, Kat.' He whispers in my ear. 'And not just anyone will do, will they? I wonder what turns you on the most? Would you like to be taken on your hands and knees like a common alley cat? Is that what would make the pussy cat roar like a lion?'

I love a man for a hard fuck. I particularly love a man who reeks of bad Tom cat. My body is clamouring. I am giddy with the stealthy sex narcotic, as it races through my bloodstream. I can smell the headiness of sex scent and hot snatch, rising into my nostrils, and I melt around his hips, a sigh of pleasure escaping my dripping, painted lips.

'Lift me onto it.' I whisper. 'Lift me onto your cock, and press me against the wall.'

I flex my wrists and lock them behind his head as he pinions me to the brickwork, my breasts pushing against his mouth. He tugs open my corset and pushing it aside, he releases first one breast and then the other. He squeezes them savagely, pressing his lips all over them. Igniting me with nips of sharp teeth.

'Is that nice, Kat?' His one hand wriggles my skirt up over my hips so he can cup my buttocks, and then with the other, he sinks his nails into my feverish flesh. It is so delicious I think I might swoon. He takes his time to linger on my nipples, stimulating them to rock-hard points. 'Only creatures come down alleys. Is that what you are, Kat? An alley Kat whore? Because you sure behave like one?'

'I love it when you talk filthy alley talk. Fuck me.' I plead. 'I want to be fucked hard up against the wall, like a dirty hooker.'

He keeps rubbing and pinching my nipples between his thumb and forefinger, and I explode in shuddering orgasmic frenzy.

Tom cat is smiling at me, a sardonic twist to his lips. 'Reach up for me, darling, and hold the fire escape.' He grasps my hips and hitches me up, so that my legs are now wrapped around his neck. My muscles scream as I stretch my arms higher, then higher still, until eventually my fingers are gripping the rusty metal.

Separating my thighs, his fingers dance over the tiny silk thong, which barely conceals my now engorged quim. He leans closer, inspecting my kitty cunt, sniffing it just like a Tom cat, his tongue poking at the silk. I squeal in delight, thrashing and moaning. I want his mouth. His fingers. His cock. Tom cat's tongue darts out and captures the sex juice on my thigh. 'Baby.' He says. 'That's some sweet pussy milk.'

He buries his head and lips between my two trembling thighs, his maw opening to take a huge mouthful of my bleeding peach. I shiver and cry. I am assailed by rapid pulsations between my legs. Electrical charges leaping from one nerve plexus to the next as he seeks the kitty cream.

'You've got the morals of an alley cat.' Then he steps back suddenly, leaving me suspended in midair.

'What do you think you're doing? You idiot!'

'I just want to admire the view.'

'Let me down.'

'Oh, I don't think so. How long do you think you could hang there, Kat?' He sidesteps my flailing legs and inserting his finger into my weeping slit, he rubs it back and forth. 'If I were to tickle your clit, do you think you would fall?'

'If you try it, I'll kill you. You shit.'

He laughs at me, his eyes lust-darkened.

I am a delectable platter ready to be sampled, as I display my pubic fuzz, and dusky raspberry red nipples, rigid with desire

Now he cannot reach my breasts, but he is level with my other mouth. 'Little pussy whore.' He snaps the elastic of my thong, revealing my scarlet slash and pouring cunt. He cannot resist caressing my silky white skin, then passing his hand over my swollen snatch. Raking his fingers through my crisp pubic hair. I stop wriggling as his mouth approaches my sex. I hold my breath in delight, I wonder if when he tries to eat me I ought to kick him with my stiletto clad feet. It would serve him right. On the other hand, I want his fat, long tongue forcing its way inside my tunnel.

Tom cat tickles me, he separates my lubricious folds with his fingers and when he finds my hyper-stimulated bud, he begins to rub and pinch until my clit is throbbing. 'Hold on tight, Kat, I would hate you to fall.' His nose and mouth titillate the now inflamed nub, before fastening his teeth onto it and sucking me as hard as he can. The sucking draws the orgasm out of me, in wave after wave of sheer unadulterated joy.

'What are you doing? don't stop.' I whimper, as withdrawing his mouth, he reaches into his pocket.

'I have a little surprise for you, Kat. I know how much you like your little toys.' And gripping my buttocks, he slides the mini vibrator out of his pocket and into my clenched anus. 'You like that don't you, babe? I can tell.'

I grip the fire escape with my arms. I am now feeling insensate from the arousal. My orgasm is circling and mounting in a wicked spiral of pleasure. But it is too far to the alley floor and I simply cannot let go, and jump to the ground.

'My, you do make a delicious spectacle hanging there.' The vibrator slips deeper into my lubed tunnel as he pushes his head between my legs to eat my slit, dancing and jabbing his tongue skilfully in and out. Flicking the stem of my clit, before once again circling the hard bud. The invading mouth on one side, and the vibrator throbbing against the thin membrane of my other hole, is too much to bear.

At the moment of trembling orgasm, he withdraws, lips moist with my pussy milk. And standing back, he watches me as I surrender. My body gives in, my limbs stretch, and I convulse in flashpoints. I wish someone would look down the alley, I wish they would bear witness to my bestial initiation. I hope the whore is staring down from her upstairs window and she feels jealous at my filthy rapture. I look up and I see the lamp glowing in the apartment and I shiver with violent excitement, as I am spot-lit from above. I tremble from the erotic charge of being observed performing on my stage, by

147

the voyeur. I never felt this sexually aroused. Tom cat is charging my desire, playing me. He steps beneath me, lowering my thighs to his shoulders, and my kitty milk drips onto his shoulder.

'Bastard. What did you do that for?'

'You didn't think I'd leave you hanging there did you.'

I watch entranced as he unzips his pants and lifts out his rigid cock. He is hard and distended. The tip swollen and wet with filthy, Tom cat lube. 'I have just the thing for that at home.' I smile wickedly. I release the fire escape, sagging into his arms and he kisses me. Deep searching kisses which tickle my palate and caress my tongue.

'I just love coming down dark alleys to jerk off.' Tom cat growls. 'They do something to me. Give me this animal instinct to fuck myself senseless. But I didn't think I'd find an on heat kitty queen to chase.'

He holds me tightly running his hands all over me, before allowing me to slowly slither down his tall body. He presses my naked thighs to his straining cock and I reach down my greedy fingers to grasp his straining shaft, sliding my long nails along the stem towards his silken, heavy balls. Savagely he grips my shoulders and forces me down. My mouth seizes him, sharp teeth nibbling, as I take his salty pole inside my mouth and work it aggressively.

I play to the secret hooker.

'Enough, wench. Get on your hands and knees.' He pushes me down until my face is inches from the ground and, beneath my palms, the echo of the alley resounds through my blood. I give small moans of ecstasy as his hands roam over my liberated body. I am oozing pussy juices from every orifice as my senses flip into overdrive, and my basic instincts magnify. Lifting me up, he spreads my legs and pinning me across an overturned dustbin, he feels once again for the eager, sucking quim.

'I've made quite a study of your dirty habits. I've watched you for ages as you rummaged amongst the rubbish from my flat. You know I really warmed to your game, Kat, so I began to plant little surprises for you amongst the detritus of my everyday life. My, my you are a dirty little kitty aren't you? Because you took them all home. In particular I remember that rather wonderful pink vagina. I wonder what you did with that? I had lots of fun imagining.' His voice is becoming progressively huskier. 'Then when I saw you become the little voyeur, my heart leapt. I thought that is the woman for me. A filthy, kitty queen to rule with me over my territory.'

'So it's you who lives above the Starlite Club? You filthy pervert!'

'You're a fine one to talk. We're rather two of a kind, aren't we?' His fingers dig deeper between my sucking kitty cunt, and I shiver as an orgasmic tidal wave erupts. At the same time his turgid Tom cat dick, is bearing down on my pussy, nudging itself into my molten tunnel. 'Meow.' He purrs in my ear, as his fingers rake my back.

Forcing aside the two ripe globes, he begins to pump his tumescent Tom cat dick violently in and out. 'This is how you really want it isn't it, Kat? I rather fancied up against the wall myself, but I really think this way is much more fitting for a real alley Kat don't you?

Red's Threesome Fantasy
by Red

It was getting late as Red turned the key in the front door to their little terraced house. "That's strange," she thought to herself. The unusually eerie silence unnerved her. "Where are Sparkie and the kids?" She stepped from the street into their lounge and closed the door, her strappy heels clanking on the wooden floor.

"Hello?" Red called out into the silence. "Where the hell was everyone?" She made her way through to the kitchen. "They must have popped out to the shop," she thought to herself. Red took a glass from the cupboard and poured herself some wine from the fridge. She was just about to take a sip when someone grabbed her roughly from behind. Her heart missed a beat and she jumped with fright, wine splashing down her arm and between her full breasts. It was Sparkie.

"Shit, you made me jump, you bastard," Red panted, her heart in her mouth. She wiped the splashes of wine from her cleavage. "Look! You made me spill it!" she chuckled. "What have you done with the kids?"

Sparkie grinned, "They're at your mum's. We're having a night just for us, like I promised we'd have. No interruptions." He gently slid his hands up the inside of Red's thighs, stopping to appreciate the delicate lace tops of her stockings and the taut silk of her suspenders. He snapped the elastic against Red's skin, making her wince. "Mmm, sexy," he said. He turned Red to face him and holding her head firmly in his hands he kissed her hard on the lips, and then gently began to explore her mouth with his hot tongue taking her breath away and leaving her panting for more. Sparkie's trousers had begun to tighten over his growing cock and Red traced the outline of it with the tip of her finger. Grabbing Red firmly around the waist he lifted her up onto the kitchen counter, forcing her legs wide apart and pressing his groin hard into hers. Red could feel Sparkie's throbbing cock against her pussy and longed to tear at his clothes, to feel him inside her, but tonight was Sparkie's night. He was in control.

Sparkie dropped to his knees and breathed in the musky smell of Red's pussy from within her silk thong. Red couldn't understand it herself, she felt sweaty and dirty having been at work all day, but Sparkie seemed to be driven wild by her scent and he buried his face into her crotch. His tongue lapped against the seam of her thong and he pulled the creamy-coloured material aside to reveal her already pink and swollen lips. He sucked each lip in turn, then gently probed deep inside Red, fucking her slowly with his tongue and making her arch her back and press her wet pussy longingly into his face. Sparkie shook his head, "No Red, we can't have you cumming just yet, I've got plans for you tonight. You've got to really want it before I'm gonna let you have it." Red grinned, she loved not being in control.

Taking Red's hand, he led her back into the lounge and told her to sit down. She did as she was told, she wasn't a very good subbie normally and often misbehaved or got the giggles and got spanked but tonight she was going to be good, "Sparkie's good girl".

A thin length of material lay on the arm of the sofa, Red hadn't noticed it there on her way in and she wondered what it was for. Sparkie picked it up and wound it tightly over Red's eyes plunging her into complete blackness and mystery. He began unbuttoning her shirt and gently removed it. Red could feel his hot breath on her breasts as he became more and more aroused. He loosened her bra and released her breasts, allowing them to hang free, so he could chew on her nipples. Red gasped with that kind of painful pleasure. She loved it when Sparkie bit her, not too hard but hard enough. It made her so horny for him.

"Get up, Red," Sparkie commanded. He pulled her roughly over to their chimney breast wall. Some weeks ago now, Sparkie had hidden a couple of eyebolts high at the back of the shelves on either side of the wall. Back then he had tied Red to them, facing their huge mirror and they had watched each other as they made love. Sparkie now had two lengths of rope and once again tied each of Red's wrists tightly, then fastened them to the eyebolts high on the shelf. He pulled the ropes tight so that Red's face was almost on the mirror and there was no escape. Sparkie tugged at Red's skirt and thong and left them round her ankles. Her pussy felt on fire as she thought of what he might do to her, standing here helpless in just her stockings, suspenders and heels, her knickers round her ankles. She prayed the curtains were closed properly and that she couldn't be seen from the street, although secretly the thought of being watched drove her wild. She'd often fantasised about having someone in the room watching while they made love, wanking themselves furiously as Sparkie took her roughly. The very thought made her pussy throb and she could feel herself getting wetter and wetter.

Sparkie left the room, the anticipation was almost becoming too much. Red could hear Sparkie chatting to someone. "Oh my God!" she thought "There's someone here." Her heart began to pound and her mouth became dry as her breathing got harder and faster. Sparkie returned and Red's heart felt as though it would explode though her chest.

"All sorted, babe," Sparkie chuckled to himself. "I just had to make a quick phone call." Red sighed, half-relieved, half-disappointed that they hadn't got company after all. Still she wondered who the hell could be so important that he needed to call them now. She could feel Sparkie standing close behind her now. She could hear him removing his clothes and she began to get all hot and excited. Sparkie pressed his huge hard cock against her arse. He was obviously as horny as hell because Red could feel the wetness of his precum on her bare cheeks. She longed for him to take her now. To ram that huge hard cock of his inside her, but Sparkie was just teasing her. He rubbed the end of his cock between her swollen pussy making it catch on her clit and moan with pleasure. Red pleaded with him to take her.

"Please, baby, give me that cock, fuck me baby, please" Red was becoming wild with passion.

"Not yet, sweetheart, I told you, you gotta want it bad baby, it's better that way." Sparkie grinned wickedly to himself. "Now be quiet or I'll have to spank you, maybe I should gag you, huh, babe?" Red lowered her head; she knew she had to behave. Sparkie always got carried away once he started to spank Red, her arse would glow pink and sore when he'd finished. She didn't want that. Or did she? Was that why she always misbehaved? Red smiled to herself.

Sparkie began rummaging in a plastic bag, Red's curiosity was getting the better of her, "What you doing, babe?" she whispered. Sparkie tutted loudly and slapped Red hard on the arse.

"Thought I told you to be quiet," Sparkie grumbled, slapping Red's bare cheeks again and again. "Now do as you're told." Red bit on her lip. She felt so horny and out of control, her cheeks tingling and pink.

"Stick your arse out for me, baby, show me that pretty little hole," breathed Sparkie. Cool oil trickled down Red's lower back, running between her cheeks and down over her twitching anus. She felt the tip of something cold and hard pressing against her hole. She tensed up with the shock then relaxed as Sparkie twisted the thin vibrator into her arse, allowing it to slip right in up to his fingers. "Now you hold that in there for me, baby, no letting it slip, you hold it nice'n'tight for me." Sparkie loved to watch Red squirming to hold onto a vibrator. He knew that with the amount of oil he used, gravity would cause it to slip and Red would pull her cheeks in desperately trying not to let it slip. The intensity of the vibrations was sending Red into frenzy. Her pussy began to drip as her juices flowed. The more she tried to stop the vibrator slipping, the more it seemed to be squeezed out.

"Oh, baby, push it in harder," Red pleaded, "I want it in deeper." Sparkie slipped the vibrator in and out of Red's arse then pushed it in deep. Red moaned. Pulling a silk scarf from his bag, Sparkie tied it tight around Red's mouth. The dryness of the material made her salivate and gag a little, but Red was enjoying her restraint. She loved to be treated mean.

"I told you! Quiet!" Sparkie barked "Now you keep this in your arse this time unless you want a good spanking."

Red did as she was told. The curtain rings clattered on their pole as Sparkie could be heard peering out into the street. "What the hell is he up to?" wondered Red for an instant. She could barely control herself and desperately wanted Sparkie to fill her other hole. There was a knock at the door. Red went into a panic. "Shit, who would it be at this time of night?" Red thought. "It could be Mum or anyone." She wasn't exactly in the position to greet guests. Red pulled furiously against her bindings and wanted to cover her naked flesh, to hide herself," She muttered into the gag, trying to get Sparkie to release her, but he could just be heard slipping back into his underwear. Sparkie went to the door and opened it. Red became wild with panic. The vibrator made a loud clatter as it slipped out of Red's arse and landed on the wooden floor. It lay there buzzing away to itself as Red gasped and struggled.

A male voice could be heard; Red recognised it but couldn't for the life of her place it. She was panting hard now, her hot breath had covered the mirror in condensation, and the gag was wet from where she had been biting on it, desperate to call out to Sparkie to untie her. She was surprised at how horny she still felt. There was something totally erotic about being so exposed, so vulnerable. Footsteps could be heard entering the door. Red froze.

"You're just in time, Folly me old mate. Your little kitten's being bad and I know how much you'd love to spank her," Sparkie laughed.

"Shit." Red squirmed. "No, it couldn't be Folly." She recognised the voice now, it was Folly. They'd never met before, but she and Sparkie had talked with him plenty of times on the web cam and they'd even put on the odd naughty show for each other. They'd met up by chance one day in a chat room, it was about six months ago and now they regularly chatted over the net. Red couldn't believe he was here. She felt her skin flush with embarrassment and excitement. She loved the games she and Folly played and now he was here, standing behind her. She could smell his aftershave and longed to see him 'in the flesh'. The picture on the web cam wasn't much to go by. All she could tell from that was that he had a huge cock. She smiled to herself.

"You're looking sexy as ever, Kitten," Folly stroked his fingers down the length of Red's spine. She shivered. "What's this?" Folly bent down to pick up the vibrator from the floor. It was still buzzing away furiously. Red could feel Folly's breath on her thighs he kissed the tops of her stocking clad legs and cupped his huge hand under her pussy. Red gasped and Folly stood up close behind her. She could feel his enormous erection pressing into her through his clothes. He slid his hand back slightly and inserted two fingers deep inside Red's swollen pussy as she moaned into her gag. He removed them and sucked each finger in turn, savouring every drop of Red's sweet and tangy juices. "Mmm, you taste fine, you don't mind if I help myself, do you, Sparkie?" Folly beamed at him.

"Go ahead mate, make my day. I'll just watch," Sparkie grinned as his got himself comfortable on the sofa.

"Something not quite right tho', Kitten" Folly said as he reached into his pocket. "Ah there it is." Folly pulled a dainty red studded collar from his pocket, he fastened it around Red's neck as tight as it would go without strangling her, then clipped a long lead onto it. "That's better, Kitten." Folly smiled at the reflection of himself and Red in the mirror. He pulled the lead taut making Red arch her neck back. This was Red's fantasy, she'd told Sparkie about it ages ago. Now it was being played out for real. Never in her wildest dreams had she thought this would happen. She was so fucking horny now; her pussy seemed to be begging to be filled.

Folly smirked "Now I hear you've been a bad girl, Kitten,

you not taking care of your toys properly? Now you better be good for me." Folly pressed the still buzzing vibrator hard onto Red's anus. She resisted at first but Folly slapped her cheeks hard and pushed harder, slipping the vibrator deep inside Red's arse. Red began to shake, as the thoughts of what was really happening sent her into orgasm after orgasm. Her nipples stood on end like huge hard cherries and her pussy juices ran down her legs. "Good girl, Red," Folly smiled. Red was smiling too. Folly continued to fuck Red's arse with the vibrator, then without warning pulled it out and switched it off. Red could hear Folly undressing and then the room was quiet and still except for the faint moisture sounds coming from Sparkie as he wanked himself on the sofa. "Let's get you down from here, Red, so I can play with you," Folly suggested. He untied Red from the wall, leaving the ropes attached to her wrists and the collar round her neck. "Now, Kitten, come with me and lay over my knee so I can see that spanked arse of yours." Red did as she was told, she staggered blindly across the room in her heels, her thong still round her ankles as Folly pulled her lead taut, making her follow him.

"Just here, Kitten, lay across my legs." Red's nipples caught on the hairs on Folly's legs and she moved herself so that they'd catch again, it felt good. Folly gently untied the gag. "Now no talking or you'll get what's coming to you." Folly laughed wickedly as he stroked his huge strong hands over Red's tingly cheeks. Red moaned, only to feel the full force of those huge hands slapping her cheeks hard. Folly loved spanking; he'd sent Red photos of his wife's bottom before. It had been red, swollen and almost bruised-looking. "Put something in her mouth again, Sparkie, keep her quiet." Sparkie shuffled along the sofa and positioned himself in front of Red's open mouth. Red gagged as Sparkie packed his huge wet cock into her throat. She lapped hungrily and began sucking hard as Sparkie groaned with pleasure. Red couldn't believe this was happening and her pussy ached with desire. Folly handed the lead to Sparkie, who pulled tight on Red's collar forcing her to take his whole cock deep in her throat.

157

Red began to reach and Folly slapped her arse hard, chastising Red for her bad behaviour. Harder and harder, Sparkie pumped into Red's mouth until at last he shot his load deep into her throat. Red gulped eagerly and swallowed it down.

Folly's cock was pressing hard into Red's belly and she longed to feel it filling her. Folly sensed her longing and, taking the lead from Sparkie pulled Red back. "Come and sit on my lap, Kitten," Folly beckoned. Sparkie moved himself to the armchair and continued to wank his still firm cock slowly, his breathing shallow and lustful, enjoying what he was seeing.

"Now let's see those eyes, Kitten." Folly loosened the blindfold and Red squinted in the light of the room, her eyes unable to focus. Then, there he was, Folly in the flesh. Red smiled and looked a little uncomfortable and apprehensive. Here she was exposed and vulnerable, straddling the naked lap of a virtual stranger. "That's not like you, Kitten, you're far from shy on the cam," smirked Folly. Red smiled a coy smile.

"Come on then, you're always talking dirty online, I know you, Red, you're just as rude as I am. You love this". He was right, Red loved this, far more than she'd ever imagined. She glanced at Sparkie, seeking his approval, she'd never been with anyone else since they married and she felt a little uneasy.

Sparkie nodded his approval, "If you want it, Red, you take it, baby, it won't change what we have." Sparkie was right; this was just lust, animal instinct if you like. It was that primitive desire deep within her soul and Red wanted it alright! She removed her thong from her ankles and knelt high above Folly's hard glistening cock. She gripped hard onto his shoulders and slid easily onto his length. Sparkie pulled hard on his own cock, his eyes wide with excitement at seeing his wife pleasured by another man.

Red let out a deep sigh. Folly felt huge and rock-hard inside her and there was nothing more Red liked than a rock-hard cock inside her. She began to ride him steadily, slowly at first feeling the full length of his shaft with each stroke. Then deeper and faster, slamming her arse cheeks hard onto Folly's lap. Folly just smiled and gripped Red's arse cheeks firmly, banging himself powerfully into her swollen mound. Red began to cum, her neck flushed, her nipples became erect and her pussy gripped Folly's cock tighter than ever. She jerked violently, her juices gushing over his cock. Folly held his breath, then as his body shook; he pumped Red's pussy full of his hot sticky cum. Red smiled breathlessly and glanced over at Sparkie. Their eyes met and there was an unspoken moment of passion between them. Sparkie was looking ecstatic and continued to pump away at his cock like a man possessed.

"Now be a good girl, Kitten, clean up this mess," Folly said sternly, giving the lead a little tug. Red lifted herself off Folly's still firm cock and got down in front on him on her knees. She began to curl her tongue around his cock, gently licking at their cocktail of juices. Sparkie couldn't take it any longer he needed to fulfil his own needs. Kneeling on the floor behind Red, Sparkie took the ends of each of the ropes on Red's wrists. He pulled her arms tight behind her back to restrain her. Sparkie then slipped a finger inside Red's pussy and used her juices to moisten her arse. Then, slowly, inch by inch, he eased his throbbing cock inside Red's twitching anus.

She gasped wide-eyed and gagged on Folly's cock. Never before had she taken two cocks, the very thought drove her wild and she pushed back against Sparkie, taking him fully inside her arse as Folly tugged hard at her collar making her take more of him in her mouth. Both men pumped away at either end of Red, packing her full of hard cock. Just when she thought she could take no more, Sparkie began to slide his fingers into her hot throbbing pussy. She was dripping wet and his fingers slipped in easily. He added more and more fingers until only his thumb remained. He began to wiggle his fingers around and stimulate Red's g-spot. Red thought she might die, her head was swimming and she felt hot and faint, but fucking fantastic. Her pussy juices flowed down Sparkie's arm, serving only to make him take her harder and faster. Folly too began to pull on Red's hair, making her fuck him with her

159

mouth until both men reached the point of no return and pumped her full of their creamy cum.

Panting and wasted Red climbed up onto the sofa and laid her head in Folly's lap. His huge cock dripping with cum brushed against her cheek. Sparkie sat besides her, stroking his hands along her hot damp and still tingling flesh. Folly brushed her wet hair back from her face. Red smiled a contented smile, her pussy was sore. She was covered in cum but she was ecstatic and had never felt so fucking horny in her life. Slowly Red drifted off to sleep, her fantasy fulfilled.

Play With Me
by Dakota Rebel

It was the final night of the play and all of us cast members were in high spirits. We'd spent two straight weeks together, rehearsing in the morning for the evening performances. We'd become a pseudo-family in this short time, but it was nice to have been with like-minded people for so long. I knew I would be sad when the curtain fell tonight, knowing that my time with these people was over. But at the same time it would be a relief to end the gruelling schedule I had put myself on.

I had been thrilled to receive the leading role in the story, and even more excited to be playing across from Tony Sherard, international star of the stage. When I auditioned I had been trying out for just a bit part, but after the director saw how well Tony and I had gotten along between scenes, he'd decided the chemistry would be perfect in front of an audience. So rather than having five lines in one scene, I had been offered the part of Ramona, concubine to Raul, who apart from having the majority of the speaking lines in the show, also had to get naked and pretend to have sex with Tony on stage in front of an audience every night and twice on Saturday.

I must admit this was not much of a hardship on my part. Tony was gorgeous. Black hair, dark skin, piercing green eyes … yeah, I can think of a million worse gigs than the one that fell in my lap that day.

But this was our final night, the last time I would ever get under the sheets with my hunky co-star. And it made me a little sad. I would miss the weight of a man on me every night, even if it had only been acting, even if he'd had his 'privacy sock' on every time we were together. It was the closest I would ever come to having sex with a celebrity ... and after tonight it would be over.

"Alright people." Cisco, the director had been frantically running around backstage, shoving cast members out of his way, screaming at the make-up and wardrobe girls, and basically being a gigantic asshole since the curtain had gone up on our final show. "This is it you two." He pointed at Tony and I who had been trying like hell to stay out of his way all night. "Your final show, the last nude scene of the play. I want it believable, you need to sell it to these people. I want people walking out of here wondering if you were actually fucking under those sheets tonight. I want the whole town talking about you two tomorrow. Got it?"

"Got it," we said together.

I looked at Tony who just grinned at me. We were both wearing robes, but within minutes we would walk naked onto the stage, meet at the bed and crawl under the sheets where his 'sock' was waiting. But I would still be uncovered and open to him.

It had been embarrassing for me the first few times, we were allowed to at least wear underwear during rehearsal, but when I had been naked and under him ... well it may be harder for a man to hide his arousal but there are signs for a woman as well. I had been terrified he would smell how wet the feel of him against me had made my pussy. Or that on the few occasions his cloth clad dick brushed me that it would become soaked with my juices. Luckily, if he ever noticed he hadn't said. And the more we did the scene, the more relaxed I became with him. Oh, I still got wet when he was on me, but there were times I got wet around him fully dressed so there was nothing I could do about that anyway.

The lights backstage dimmed a few times, announcing that our scene was coming up. I took a deep breath and dropped the robe, turning to watch Tony do the same next to me. He grinned at me then kissed my forehead.

"You'll be great. Don't worry. And after tonight you'll never have to deal with my accidental erections again."

I watched him walk away, stunned into silence by his words. I had never noticed him getting hard for me before. I must have been too preoccupied with my own situation. Damn, it would have been nice to know before tonight that he had been turned on by the scene as well.

I ran to the wings to take my mark, not wanting to miss the cue on closing night and face the wrath that was Cisco for it. I caught Tony wink at me from across the stage and the music started. We walked onto the stage, meeting in the centre where he took my hands in his and stared down into my eyes.

"Ramona," he said, his voice more hoarse than I had ever noticed before. "Tonight you will be mine, I will take you to my bed and I will mark you as my equal, my love, my Queen."

"Raul," I said, noticing that my voice had a shake to it tonight. "Tonight I will take you inside me as I have done a hundred times before. But this time let it be the beginning of our forever."

OK, so the dialogue sucked. I hadn't taken the part to impress anyone, I just needed a few more credits on my resume before I headed off for New York. I was hoping that the play, even though Tony was in it, would be far enough off the map that it wouldn't come back to haunt me later.

We climbed into the bed with Tony crawling over me as he had done so many times before. He reached between us, I assumed to find the sock that was hidden there, but I had to stifle a gasp when his finger played up the slit of my pussy instead. He met my eyes with a small smile and I returned it, wondering what he was doing but not wanting to ruin the scene.

I could feel the familiar wetness between my legs, but this time I did notice that Tony was aroused too. His cock had grown full and hard against my thigh, his pre-cum burning on my skin where it trailed when he moved.

Fortunately the scene had no lines, just a few sighs and

moans where we felt appropriate. When his finger started to make hard circles over my clit I knew that I would never have remembered any words if I'd had to say them anyway.

I felt him slide something down his cock and sighed, thinking he had put the sock on and was done messing with me for the night. I thought it had probably just been closing night antics, something I had been warned about from other cast members with more stage acting experience.

So I was shocked when he dropped down to whisper in my ear.

"Don't worry, I brought a condom."

I felt my eyes widen in surprise, before I could whisper back to him, to say yes or no or ask what the fuck he was thinking, he raised himself up with his palms on the mattress and slid inside me.

My back arched in surprise, the feel of him stretching my pussy open with his impressive cock momentarily making me forget that we had an audience. My fingers gripped into the sheets as my eyes squeezed shut and a low, guttural moan escaped my lips.

When I opened my eyes my head was turned toward the crowd and even through the haze of the stage lights I could see people in the front row talking amongst themselves. Well, Cisco had wanted us to sell it and these people were apparently going to get a hell of a show.

My face flushed with embarrassment as I realized that I was having sex on stage in front of more than a hundred strangers. I knew that I had no choice but to go on with it now, and it wasn't as if fucking Tony Sherard was a bad thing, but if I'd had to choose how it happened I don't think it would have been in public.

He was moving faster now, slamming himself inside me harder than I'd been fucked in a long time. His hands were gripped in the top sheet, holding it tightly so that it wouldn't slip off and announce to the auditorium that we were no longer acting.

The scene was only supposed to be about five minutes

long, and judging from the forcefulness of his movements he didn't plan on it taking any longer than that tonight. That was fine with me. I was already so close to coming I didn't know how I was going to control myself for much longer.

Tony shifted his hips, the new angle causing the head of his cock to rub over and over that sweet spot inside me so quickly that stars were starting to appear in my vision. His face dropped down to mine and his mouth captured my lips, forcing them apart with his tongue, kissing me as if feeding from me.

He moved his mouth down my jaw, moving toward my ear so he could whisper to me again.

"Do you like me fucking you in front of all of these people? I've dreamed about the smell of your pussy for weeks. Every night I've wanted to do this to you. Fuck you, feel your tight pussy gripping my cock, take you right here on stage."

His words caused things low in my body to constrict, and he growled when I clenched down on his cock. One, two, three more thrusts inside me and the world exploded.

I screamed, clawing at his arms and no longer caring that we had an audience, that all of these people probably knew we really were fucking up on that stage in front of them. All I cared about was the feel of his cock inside me, his breath hot on my ear, his chest heaving and his own rhythm faltering as he came close to coming for me … because of me.

He didn't last much longer, his body stiffening over mine, moaning as he filled the condom so forcefully I could feel it hot and thick as if the latex wasn't even there. He collapsed on top of me, his breathing erratic as he dropped a few awkward kisses on any part of my skin he could find.

The usual polite applause we usually received at the end of that scene became a roar through the audience. My face flushed again as I turned to see that the people had risen to their feet in a standing ovation this play had never deserved. There were cat-calls and howls from the room and if possible my face grew even hotter in embarrassment.

I turned back to Tony when he started struggling under the sheet. He gave me a small smile before climbing out of the

165

mattress with a hand out to help me as well. I couldn't help a quick glance down at his cock and smiled at the thought that he had to have left the condom on the bed. I could only hope he would retrieve it before the prop guys dismantled the set.

We took our bows and walked as casually as we could offstage, accepting our robes from a teary-eyed Cisco in the wings. The curtain fell and the applause and shouts from the crowd grew even louder.

"Get out there!" Cisco was beaming at us both. "That's your curtain call."

Tony took my hand again and led me out to the centre of the stage where the curtain came back up to show the audience still on their feet. We gave a few more bows and headed back to the wings to join the rest of the cast.

"That was amazing," Cisco said hugging us both and giving us wet kisses on our cheeks. "You two have been holding out on me."

The rest of the cast walked past, shaking our hands and murmuring their approval at our 'acting skills' as they headed off to the wrap party Cisco had arranged. We promised to meet up with them later and one by one everyone left. I sighed in relief as I headed to my dressing room and saw that Tony was indeed going to remove all evidence of our tryst from the stage.

I dressed quickly, for some reason not wanting to be naked when Tony came to my room. Which I knew he would. And a few minutes later the small knock on the door let me know I was right.

He opened the door before I could answer him, and that was fine. He'd just had his cock inside me, there wasn't much modesty I could pretend to have any more.

"I hope you're not mad at me," he said softly, shutting the door behind him.

"No, not at all. I was a little surprised, but no. It was nice." I felt like an idiot. I had no idea what to say to him now. I mean honestly, what do you say to a man you have sex with for the first time in front of a room full of people? Someone

166

should write a book about that.

"Good. I really like you. I realize that I probably should have warned you, or even asked you. But I don't know. It just seemed like the right thing to do. You know, close the show with a ... bang."

I laughed. He was just as nervous as I was, and for some reason that made the situation better. I held out my hand and he took it, laying a light kiss on it before letting go.

"Tony, it was perfect. Something I will never forget. Do you think they know?"

"The audience, or the cast?"

"Everyone."

"No. Oh, they'll wonder for the rest of their lives if they just saw us have actual sex or if we are just great actors. But no, I don't think they know for sure."

I nodded, relieved that it wouldn't get back to my family that I'd fucked a man on stage in front of an audience. As if I wasn't mortified enough at having done it, and enjoyed it, I didn't need people knowing for sure that it had happened.

"Well, are you going to the party?" he asked.

"Yeah, I thought I might stop by and say goodbye. You?"

"Well, I don't usually, but sure. Can I give you a ride?" He winked and I laughed.

I was glad that the situation didn't feel awkward between us. I knew that I would probably never see him again, but I didn't think I would ever be sorry that it had happened. Memories are half the fun of doing stupid things anyway.

"Yes, I would love a ride."

Merrilee And The PM
by Eleanor Powell

'Hey Merrilee, remember me?' Pete asked, coming up behind her and planting a kiss on the back of her neck. 'You're supposed to be married to me not that computer.'

'Oh darling, please don't be a grouch,' she said coaxingly. 'Just let me see what this email is from Spanking Swingers.'

'Ok, let's see together,' Pete lifted his long leg astride the chair she was sat on. 'Hutch up a bit,' he said.

Merrilee could feel something sticking into her back. She wriggled against it feeling his hardness. 'What's making you so horny?' she laughed.

'I can't imagine,' he said, putting his arms around her, cupping her pert breasts in his big hands.

'Ouch,' she squealed as he tweaked her nipples. He laughed.

'Go on then, click on the link,' he said.

With a couple of clicks, they were on the Spanking Swingers Site.

'Right, I got to log in,' she said. 'My User Name is … ' She suddenly stopped dead. 'I can't remember my User Name,' she wailed.

'Merrilee, you idiot,' he said standing up. 'Maybe a warm bottom will improve your memory.'

Pulling her off the chair they had just been sharing, while holding onto her wrist, he turned the chair around – sitting down on it, he pulled her over his knee.

Raising his right arm, he brought his large hand down on her upturned right bottom cheek – quickly followed by his hand landing on her left cheek.

'Owwwwwwwww!' she shrieked. 'That bloody hurt.'

Putting his mouth close to her ear, 'Guess what?' he whispered. 'It was meant to.'

'This is so unfair,' she protested. 'It's any excuse to spank me.'

'It's for your own good. I'm just helping you to improve your memory.'

'Piss off,' she said.

'Merrilee, using language like that to me is never a good idea, especially when you're in that position.' He flipped up the back of her dress, revealing virginal white satin knickers. Running his hands over her bottom cheeks, he said, 'You sure know how to turn a man on, don't you, darling?'

His right hand was busy smoothing out the wrinkles in her satin knickers. He pulled them up until they were taut across her bum cheeks. Then his fingers tucked her panties into the crack between her cheeks. As he carried on pushing the material into her extremely wet pussy, she was squirming about over his knee.

Then without warning, he again raised his right arm and brought his hand down on the top of her thigh. 'Not there, not there,' she shouted.

'Ok, is this better?' he brought his hand down in the dead centre of her quivering bottom cheeks. 'And here's another to match the other.'

'Hell! You're a sadist,' Merrilee wriggled and writhed over his knee.

'And you have masochistic tendencies, my darling,' he retorted. 'Otherwise you wouldn't keep needing a spanking.'

'As if?' she said.

'Have you remembered your User Name yet?'

'I can't think straight while you're spanking me,' she said, renewing her efforts to escape his stinging hand.

'You can protest all you want, my sweet, but being spanked

170

turns you on big time,' he said.

'No it doesn't.'

'Hmmm! So why are my trousers getting so wet?'

'Not my fault if you're not potty trained yet,' she laughed. 'Owwww! You lousy rotten sod,' she said, as he landed another six spanks on her hot tingling bottom.

His big hard hand had stopped spanking her. Now he was gently rubbing her hot cheeks. 'Let's get these out of the way,' he said, hooking his finger into the waistband of her knickers and pulling them down to her ankles – then right off. He tossed the scrap of white satin across the room.

His finger slipped easily into her very wet pussy and, finding her clit, he began to stroke it.

'Oh, Pete,' she gasped. 'I'm going to come, but it feels so strange. I-I nearly passed out just then,' she tried to explain. 'And I think I have just pissed myself.'

Pete laughed. 'You're such an innocent, aren't you? I just found your G Spot.'

'I didn't know I'd lost it,' she laughed. 'But, wow! Can you find it again?

'Yes of course, but not now.' He went back to rubbing on her engorged clit, with what she called, his magic vibrating finger.

She was soon bucking about over his knee. 'I'm coming, I'm coming,' she shouted as she felt the waves of her orgasm take over her body, leaving her shuddering and shaking.

When it was over, she lay limply over his knee.

She became aware of his stiff cock sticking into her side. She could feel it throbbing. 'Are you trying to make a new hole?' she asked.

Pete laughed. 'Come on, don't just lie there, I need a bit of loving too.' He helped her to her feet.

She knelt down between his legs. With practiced fingers, she unzipped his trousers and released his rampant cock. It stuck out from his flat belly, pulsing and swaying about. Putting her hot little mouth over the purple helmet, she opened her mouth as wide as she could – covering his manhood with

171

her mouth.

She loved sucking her lollipop. Her tongue licked down the length of his cock, then back up again, she pointed it, licking and sucking at the tip of his cock, he moaned with pleasure, while his battering ram swelled even more in her mouth.

Her fingers were also busy, gently squeezing his balls. He withdrew his cock from her mouth. Pulling her up off her knees, he pushed her over the back of the chair that he had just vacated and came all over her still sore red-hot bottom. She let out a loud sigh of relief, at the cooling effect his cum had on her stinging bottom.

'Stay right where you are,' Pete instructed her. 'I'll go get a wipe to clean you up.'

He smoothed the moist baby wipe over her rosy red cheeks. 'That feels so good,' she said.

'Right, that's you spanking new again,' he laughed giving her a slap on her upturned bottom.

'Now what were we doing before we got side tracked?' He stood her up.

'Wasn't anything important,' she said. 'It'll keep.'

She moved towards the bedroom, calling out over her shoulder, 'Come on lover boy, let's go play some more.'

'Merrilee, you're insatiable,' he laughed.

'Are you objecting?'

'God, no.' He chased her into the bedroom.

Two hours later, she came out of the bedroom, yawning and stretching – with a happy smile on her face.

She went back to the computer, sitting down gingerly. 'Ouch!' she jumped up, rubbing her sore bottom.

Going to the couch, she saw her discarded knickers lying there. 'So that's where they went,' she muttered to herself. Stepping into her white satin panties, she rolled them up over her hips, wincing as the satiny material hurt her sore bottom.

Quickly, she took them off again. Grabbing a cushion, she sat down at the computer again.

She clicked the Enter key to clear the screen saver – the

cursor was still blinking, waiting for her to type in her User Name. Suddenly, she remembered it. A sore bottom sure worked wonders. Great, now she was getting somewhere.

'Uh huh, now what did I use as a password?'

She tried her date of birth, no joy. Having no better luck with Pete's date of birth – she then noticed in small letters, 'If you have forgotten your password Click here'. After clicking as per instructions, she was asked to type in her email address and her mother's maiden name.

She was then told an email was on its way to her. When she checked her Inbox five minutes later, sure enough the promised email was waiting for her.

Her password turned out to be their wedding anniversary. I'd better not let Pete know that I forgot it or I'll never hear the end of it, she thought.

Now she was getting excited. She was almost in. Soon she'd be able to read the response from 'Adventurous Couple Into Spanking'.

She read the Private Message from Mike and Jayne. They sound so friendly, she thought. Wow! They wanted to meet her and Pete as soon as possible.

She printed out the PM.

Going into the bedroom, she looked down at the man lying on the bed, his arms outflung, a peaceful look on his handsome face, his black hair tousled and stuck up on end, 'I love you so much,' she said aloud.

'Come back to bed darling,' he murmured sleepily.

'Got something to show you,' she waved the print-out of the PM under his nose.

'Stop waving it around,' he squinted up at her. 'I'm trying to read it.'

'Open your eyes then,' she taunted him.

'Why didn't I think of that? 'Remind me to give you a spanking for being such a smart arse.'

'Promises, promises,' she laughed, sitting down on the bed.

He propped himself up on one elbow as she held out the PM to him.

His fingers were walking up the inside of her thigh, so that she was having great difficulty concentrating and holding the paper still at the same time.

Unnoticed the PM fluttered onto the bed, forgotten by both of them.

Gently he pushed her down – his walking fingers carried on walking up and down the inside of her thighs. She could feel her pussy juicing up as his finger lightly made contact with her throbbing clit. Teasing her, he withdrew his finger and let it walk back down her leg again.

'I hate you,' she told him.

'Of course you do, you tell me often enough.'

Getting off the bed, he went to the foot of it – nudging her thighs apart, His wandering digit wandered into her pussy. He gently flicked her clit, making it throb even more.

Then going down on his haunches, he replaced his finger with his tongue. Licking, sucking and gently biting her clit; she was moaning, while pushing her pussy upwards to meet his mouth.

Putting his hands under her bottom, he lifted her hips until her legs were resting over each of his shoulders.

'Oh my God!' she shrieked as her juices flooded again. 'You bugger, you've found my G Spot again.'

'I don't hear you objecting,' he said.

'I hated it, do it again.'

'You're a right Contrary Mary,' he said. 'Come on let's send a PM back to Jayne and Mike,'

'Ok, are we going to do it together?' she asked.

'We are,' he said. Standing up, he took hold of her hand and led her out of the bedroom.

She sat down in front of the computer, with him behind her, sharing the chair.

Starting to type, she wrote: Dear Jayne and Mike 'Whoa,' Pete said. 'That's far too stuffy.'

'Would Dear Sir or Madam be better?' she asked cheekily.

'Any more remarks like that, young lady, and you'll be over my knee, saying thank you Sir after each spank.'

174

'Sod off,' she said.

With language like that, I owe you a spanking,' he promised her. 'But for now, let's get on with this PM.'

After a few stops and starts, Merrilee read their joint effort aloud.

Hi Jayne and Mike

It was great hearing from you. We would love to meet you too. As you say, you can't accommodate, so you'll be very welcome to come over here. Maybe we can chat – get to know each other better before we meet. Our phone number is 123 4567 or better still we can, if you wish, chat online. Our nickname is, merripete@livetalk.com

'Does that sound OK darling?' she asked him.

'Yes, my sweet, come on send it off.'

She tapped on the Enter key.

'Wonder how long it'll be before we hear from them,' she said.

'Time enough for me to give you that spanking I promised you.'

'You'll have to catch me first,' she giggled, while still squirming about in the chair.

'This is not like you, being a sitting target.' He laughed. 'Oh well, as I don't have to waste energy chasing after you, come on out of that chair, I'm going to need it.' Taking hold of her arm, he yanked her out of it. Then sitting down, he hauled her over his lap.

She lay draped over his knee, head hanging down. 'I think we should get a new carpet,' she said.

He stopped, his arm in mid air. 'Now, what's going through that pretty head of yours?'

'Well, I do so much carpet studying, I'm bored with this carpet.'

'Is that all?' he asked. 'Here's something to look at.' He tossed a glossy magazine on to the carpet, almost under her nose.

'Hey, that's my Janus you're throwing around,' she protested.

'Hmmm! My mistake,' he said. 'I shouldn't be distracting you from what's happening.'

'Why, what's happening? Owww! You louse,'' as he brought his big hard hand down, again and again, on her bouncing reddened cheeks.

The Nerd Herd
by Sommer Marsden

I stared at the error message and tried not to scream. I hit the mouse again. Clicked randomly over the screen. Put my head down and gnashed my teeth. Nothing. The computer was completely useless. And me with a deadline.

I dialled my cell, fighting back the tears that threatened. I wasn't worried I had lost today's work. I had just backed up my data on CD before eating my lunch. I was worried that I was staring at a two thousand dollar paperweight and not a back-up computer in sight.

"Deb!" I barked, "What's the name of those guys you use? The computer guys. The Geek something?"

"Uh-oh," my best friend giggled. "Problem?"

"I have just suffered a terminal fatal error or something and my computer is frozen. Now what's the name of the company?" I was doing my best not to yell.

"I take it you have a deadline for your edits?" More snickering.

I think I growled.

"OK, OK, hold on. The company is the Nerd Herd and the number is ..." I could hear her pages ruffling. "Ah! Well, I should have remembered that. The number is 1-800-NRD-HERD"

"Thanks," I sighed and hung up. Hell, even I should have remembered that from their commercials.

I made the call, tried not to scream at the operator as I explained that this truly was an emergency and I needed someone here immediately and not a moment later. Then I sat back and chewed my fingernails waiting for my own personal nerd to arrive.

What they really needed to do was get a bunch of hunky men and send them out on calls. They could call them the *Steam Team*. I was busy coming up with stupid names for a roving band of handsome men when the doorbell rang. I reminded myself to add "Go out on a date" to my to-do list.

I steeled myself to not giggle at the impending nerd in the required outfit. The company actually made their employees dress as they are portrayed in the televisions ads. Poor thing, I thought, as if it's not bad enough to actually be a nerd, let alone be forced to dress like a cliché.

I flung open the door and nearly gasped. Yeah, he was dressed like a nerd. Too short black pants, white socks, black lace-up shoes. He even had the short sleeve, white button down and the pocket protector. And the glasses, with tape! But oh Mother Mary, he was the furthest thing from a nerd I had ever seen. I read his name tag. Tony. Tony was my own personal nerd. With big biceps and deep brown eyes and lips that made me want to …

"Ma'am?"

"Yes!?" Damn. I sounded like I'd been sucking the helium out of a party balloon. I cleared my throat and tried again. "I'm sorry. Come in, um, Tony. The computer is in the den."

I pointed a finger, seemingly frozen on the spot, and he followed my asinine directions to the den. It was only after his perfectly formed ass rounded the corner and he was out of sight, that I realized I was still in giant grey sweatpants, a yellow tank top and my wildly abused fuzzy bunny slippers.

I groaned out loud when I saw my tank sported a coffee stain.

"Ma'am, are you OK?" he called.

And a gentleman, too. Double groan.

"Fine!" I yelped and then I bolted upstairs. I threw on my low slung jeans and a T-shirt that said GEEKS LOVE ME. Then I reconsidered. Then I figured, screw it.

He was working on my computer when I entered. "These

178

things really aren't as bad as the computer indicates," he said without looking up. Then he did look up. His eyes grazing first the juvenile print screen and then the braless breasts underneath. "That true?" he asked, indicating the slogan.

I stuck my chest out further and said, "For the most part."

What the hell was I doing? Was I that desperate for male attention? I did a mental review. Last date two months ago. Last sexual encounter, sadly, two and a half months ago. Yes, I was that desperate. On my own terms, obviously. Tony fit my terms.

I took a step toward him and tried to breathe deeply. I couldn't keep my eyes still. They skittered over his broad shoulders that strained against his too tight T-shirt. Dark hair cut short and neat. Nice jaw with just a hint of stubble. The stubble sealed the deal.

I was pleased to note that his eyes were just as busy. Skimming the small swatch of skin that was exposed between the waistband of my jeans and the hem of my T-shirt. I watched them run languidly over my hips and travel down my long legs. The look in his eyes felt as intense as if his hands were on me and my white cotton thong got a quick and sudden bath as my body responded to that look.

"How long do you average per job?" I asked, my voice a little breathy.

"About an hour and a half." He gave me a smile that sort of made his top lip crinkle just a bit. My nipples went hard.

"How long is this job, do you think? Roughly speaking?" I moved closer to him.

"Less than an hour," he said. He looked up at me from my own computer chair, then spun the seat so that our knees nearly touched. That smile started to blossom just a little more.

I noticed he wasn't lagging behind me in the arousal department because those snug geek pants sheathed a beautiful bulge. He caught me looking and gave a soft laugh. He patted one broad thigh and stared me dead in the eye. I laughed, too, and then settled onto his lap before I could reconsider. Had I lost my mind? Apparently, so, but what a way to go. I couldn't resist rubbing my ass against his cock as I shifted to find a comfortable perch.

"Now that is just fighting dirty," he growled and cinched me tight around my waist, big hands splaying over the naked skin of my belly. It was my turn to growl.

His lips found the back of my neck and he kissed a trail down to my nape. I shivered then jumped in his arms as his hand slid beneath my waistband. His long lean fingers hovering just an inch or so shy of where I really wanted them to be.

"Now who's fighting dirty?" I sighed and wiggled my ass again. Pushing and grinding against his erection.

"You win." His fingers found my clit and stroked lightly. I sort of puddled in his arms. How could I have forgotten to do this? How could I have neglected myself so terribly? The questions vanished as he slowly circled my clit again and then, sliding his hand down further, hooked two big fingers into my already twitching pussy.

I splayed across his lap like a hussy and whimpered.

"That feel good?" he chuckled.

"Huhhhhhhhh," I said. Whatever the hell that meant.

A few more delicate and deliberate strokes and my body demanded more. I yanked open my top desk drawer, found a foil packet and slithered out of my jeans. I opened the packet. Tony reached for it.

"No," I said and turned on his lap. I freed his cock and tried not to whoop victoriously. His cock was long and broad. The perfect tip nearly purple. It strained against my hand. "Enthusiastic, isn't it?" I laughed.

Tony could only nod because I couldn't resist taking one long stroke against his skin with my fist before I rolled the condom on. I turned in the chair, my knees braced inside the leather arms and sank down onto him as slowly as I could bear.

He groaned and shoved my shirt up, sucking first one tightly beaded nipple, then the other. "You are the best customer ever," he sighed and we both laughed.

It wouldn't take much. I could feel my body coiling for release. Each time I sank down on him, I grew tighter. Each movement more pleasurable. He was with me, too, I could feel his body jerk up to meet mine as his big hands roamed my ass. He gave me a brisk slap on my ass cheek and that did it. My pussy clenched and groped for each last blip of pleasure it could grab as I came. Moisture wet my thighs with each spasm. Tony thrust up against me, smacking me once more. He kissed me as he came, his tongue as demanding as his cock. His big hands anchoring me to him.

We sat together panting as he feathered his nice long fingers over my nipples. I shivered. Then rested my forehead against his. He surprised me by giving me a long slow kiss before I grabbed my jeans and slid them on.

"Love that T-shirt," he said gruffly as I pulled it over my breasts.

"If you come back again, I'll wear a different one for you." I couldn't help but smile.

"What's that one say?"

"Nerds Rock My World."

Leading Lady
by Alex Severn

Thirty-five today. Maria could hardly dispute the calendar but inside, she knew she was really 22. She stopped checking her e-mails and her mind began to float into a whole series of what-ifs.

What if she had gone around the world when Kim had wanted her to? What if she had married Mike when she had the chance and not ended up with Neil? What if she …

"Morning, birthday girl. Let's have a look at your cards then."

Terri was the closest colleague she had in the office, much more than a colleague, a proper friend. A couple of years younger than Maria, she attracted more interest from the men in the office than Maria, but then the short skirts and low cut blouses helped. Maria stopped herself, Terri had supported her when she needed it, and anyway she couldn't help but notice a rather flashy-looking card in her hand.

"Here it is then. Not just a card but a present as well."

Maria tried to hide her disappointment. So there was a gift voucher or a token inside. Wonderful. Terri normally had more imagination than that and, this particular birthday, Maria really needed something expensive and pointless to cheer her up.

Smile firmly in place, she opened the card. It was filthy, no change there then but inside was an oblong shaped, scarlet coloured envelope. Funny token, she thought.

Feeling Terri's eyes on her, she slid the flap open and read the stiff card inside.

FREE ENTRY TO ONE NIGHT AT THE SCARLET
CINEMA CLUB.
MAKE YOUR DREAMS COME TRUE
BE A STAR FOR A NIGHT.
STRICTLY ADULTS ONLY.

An address she vaguely knew was given at the bottom.

"Thank you, I..I've never heard of this place, what exactly
…"

"Oh no, I'm not spoiling the surprise. Let's just say that I
have a friend who has a friend, etc. You've always fancied
amateur dramatics. Well, now you can indulge yourself. And
spice up your life as well."

With a truly filthy giggle, she was gone, leaving Maria to
wonder.

Well, she had to go. A present is a present after all. She had a
horrible feeling that she had been sent to a porn cinema society
but Terri had more class than that. She also had lots of money
and was very generous with gifts so it couldn't be a cheap
night out.

Maria had to descend a short flight of stairs from the street
to a scarlet painted door. The brass plate looked expensive and
somehow professional. An attractive young woman let her in
and showed her to what looked a reception area of a hotel.
Almost immediately a middle-aged woman who looked
disconcertingly like Prunella Scales arrived and asked, very
politely, for her admittance details.

She went into what was clearly a well-rehearsed speech to
explain what it was all about.

In essence, Maria was to choose one of three scenarios to
take part in as, in effect, a leading lady. But she was only
given sketchy details of the way the scene would go. Her
fellow 'actors' had the same details but it was her show, she
was a kind of director and could influence the proceedings.
She had one hour, after which the entertainment stopped.
Costumes were provided for all.

Almost anything went but there were a couple of fixed

rules. No violence, nobody gets hurt, and she could stop the show anytime she liked by the use of a single codeword which would be enclosed with the envelope of whichever scenario she decided on. Did she understand? Yes, she did.

She actually began to shiver with anticipation as 'Prunella' handed her the three envelopes. Yes, of course they were scarlet.

The first one was a Viking drama. Maria would be a Saxon maiden in a village near the coast when the marauding hordes swept in. In her scene, she tried valiantly to fight off a particularly blond, particularly muscular, Viking, who carried her off and kept her as his plaything. Sounds promising, she thought.

The second was set in Roman times and revolved around a mini-orgy (perhaps the budget didn't stretch any further). The details seemed a little lame to Maria.

But the third one somehow struck a chord. She would be the Khadine, the Sultan's favourite wife. A new young girl had been brought to their palace and she was to help him decide if he would keep her. There was a final note:

The actor playing the sultan is 25, with the body of an athlete and of genuine Jordanian descent. Maria had always been turned on by Arabian looking men and the choice was a simple one.

She was shown to where she could change, given a costume by an uninterested looking girl, and minutes later was admiring herself in the full-length mirror provided.

Maria saw herself wearing a robe, a very tiny bra and an almost sheer pair of loose trousers with an embroidered band that tapered to a V at the front and the back. The trousers fitted very low on her hips, exposing her navel, and exposure was very much the theme of the upper half of her body. The delicate robe was little more than a couple of skimpy strips of chiffon attached to narrow satin ribbons. She actually looked more provocative than if she had been completely naked and she felt a thrill of excitement as she went through the door that had been pointed out to her.

The lights were dimmed low on her side of the room but the far end was lit by a series of spotlights and Maria saw a small podium. As she turned her head to the right, she saw her 'sultan'. He was cross-legged on the floor and, even in the dim light, she could see he was darkly handsome, looking younger than his 25 years. He was wearing a black velvet robe from his chin to his feet, fastened at the throat by a large, crown-shaped ornament, with what must have been fake emeralds. He beckoned her to sit next to him, and, knowing she would be able to see him better, she was happy to oblige.

But before she had actually settled next to him, a figure entered the room and stood under the spotlights. Both Maria and her sultan watched as the young girl began to dance.

She must have been in her teens, with long blonde hair falling onto her shoulders. She was wearing a tan-coloured bikini that left little enough to the imagination. Her neck and wrists were liberally covered in jewellery that glinted as she swayed her body to the eastern rhythms that were now being piped through to them. Maria had read that belly-dancing was great for keeping fit and this girl could have been the teacher, given her age and the firm, well-proportioned body, any dance movements would have been easy for her.

The girl began to run her hands over her breasts and then she ran her fingers along the inside of her thighs. Maria half turned and saw the excitement and arousal in the sultan's eyes. She had to admit she was being turned on by his reactions. Or was she also aroused by the girl herself? She would never have dreamt that seeing a young woman posing and pouting in front of her would excite her, but it certainly did. Her admiration was laced with envy towards a kid who was probably young enough to be her daughter, but her emotions were running this show, not her head.

Instinctively, she reached out and allowed her left hand to stray between her male companion's legs, and her heart quickened to feel, even through the velvet of his robe, his growing hardness. He jerked his head towards her and she was rewarded with a deep smile and a flash of eyes that were

186

almost black. She wanted to touch him properly so she moved her right hand to the hem of the robe and lifted it up towards his stomach. She was delighted, although not surprised, to find he was naked underneath and in seconds her left hand was caressing the tip of his spectacularly large penis, while her right hand was alternately squeezing him around his balls, then circling his shaft. Maria was gasping herself at how she was controlling him with her hands and was astonished and disappointed when, with a sudden, almost violent movement, he moved backwards, pushing both her hands away with his own.

Her disappointment was short-lived however, as the sultan eased her shoulders backwards and literally ripped the delicate fabric of her trousers off her body, exposing her to him completely. She heard him breathing heavily as his hand moved between her legs and he began stroking her labia. Maria had a thick bush of hair, she prayed he was turned on by that. She had already started to moisten when she had been touching him but she eagerly opened her legs wider to allow his probing fingers deeper inside her passage. She managed to manoeuvre herself back into a position from where she could resume her coaxing and stroking, but then, with an almost psychic co-ordination, they both turned to see the dancer who had now removed her bikini top, showing off her perfectly shaped, small breasts. She began to lick her fingers and massage her nipples, fixing them both with a look of intense passion and longing. With a quick movement, she turned her back on them, her hair flowing almost halfway down her spine. Maria and her fellow voyeur paused in their massaging of each other, as if they needed to fully focus on the girl. She bent her supple body forward, pushing out her bottom. The bikini bottom was virtually just a thong, tied with delicate strings; she quickly untied both sides, and pulled it off between her legs. Straightening up again, she paused briefly, as if knowing she had her audience exactly where she wanted them. Then a sudden twirl of movement and she was facing them again, naked and glistening with sweat. Maria couldn't prevent a gasp of pleasure escaping from her throat as the sultan's fingers were now massaging her clitoris, her wetness pouring out.

Maria observed that, in complete contrast to herself, the dancer had shaved her pubic hair, it excited and aroused Maria in a way she would never have thought possible. With the confidence that only the very young and the very beautiful ever have, the dancer walked towards the couple and paused, a couple of yards away, still standing. As if answering Maria's deepest wish, she began to touch herself, stroking, massaging until Maria could see her lips raised and damp. The lack of any hair seemed to make her more vulnerable, her labia resembled rosebud petals, and it was as if her most intimate parts were aflame with desire.

For a few seconds, everything froze. The sultan and the dancer half turned towards Maria and then she realised. She was the leading lady, the director. They were waiting for their instructions from her!

Maria pulled off what was left of her clothes, eased herself forward and knelt on all fours just in front of the sultan. Lowering her upper body towards the floor, she turned her head, stared straight into his eyes and inched her body even nearer to him. As she turned back, she glimpsed his powerful muscular chest, dripping with sweat, simply heightening her determination to have him deep inside her, probing her. He didn't need words to tell him what she wanted and, as he moved nearer her, she felt his rock-hard penis brush lightly against her buttocks. Then, he was inside her, driving, sliding deeper and deeper. She was so aroused that he could slide deep inside her easily. She began to gasp as he managed to pull out of her and then roughly enter her again. Only once before had a man taken her from behind, it was years ago when she was at university during a drunken and ultimately unfulfilling night. God, could this get any better?

Maria looked straight up at the dancer and realised that there was a way of making this even more fantastic. Beckoning the girl to kneel down, directly in front of her,

Maria steadied herself with one hand, freeing up the other. First, she reached up to the girl's left nipple and shivered as she felt it was as hard as glass. She traced her finger all round it, bringing a moan of pleasure. She ran one finger up the thigh of the dancer and then with a quick movement felt inside her already soaking passage. Feeling the girl actually moving onto her, she brought another finger around to feel her lips, further and further inside. She felt the hard nub of her clitoris with her thumb and forefinger and she began to synchronise her plunging fingers with the driving shaft of the sultan's penis, she caught sight of the girl's face, transfixed with pleasure. A particularly savage thrust caused her to slip slightly and she had to put both hands on the floor to avoid falling over. A glance at the girl's face told her how desperate she was for this not to stop, her mouth opened to plead with her to carry on but Maria was just as keen to explore her as she was to be explored.

Maria knew she was close to the most fabulous orgasm now and began to panic. She was praying he could keep this going, the thought of him softening and shrinking inside her body too awful.

She rocked herself back onto him, still delving deeper and deeper into her female partner's lips, and then, in a moment she would never forget, she came, gloriously, waves of sheer primitive pleasure breaking over her. The dancer pushed her away weakly, signalling that she too had reached her climax.

The sultan made it a perfect trio and for a few seconds nobody moved, buried in their own fantasies.

Then, almost together, her two companions sat up and left the room by a door near the podium. Maria looked up at the clock and saw there was one minute left of her time. Self-conscious now, as if the world could see her, she gathered up what little clothes she had come in with and went to get changed into the blouse and jeans that took her back to reality.

As she went back into reception, 'Prunella' was there, all smiles and knowing looks.

"Here you are, a tape of your evening. Didn't you notice

189

the camera?"

Maria's face must have been easy to read because she added, "Don't worry, love, this isn't a blackmail racket. This is the only tape there is. You can destroy it when you get home. Of course, you might want to watch it with a loved one."

Crossing the road to the multi-storey, Maria was still smiling. Well, Neil was always saying there's nothing to watch on the TV. Perhaps he might get a surprise one of these nights.

The True Confessions of a London Spank Daddy

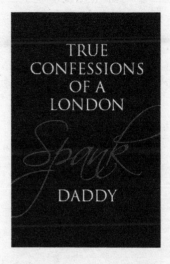

My name is Peter, I'm 55 and I'm a Spank Daddy. I offer a spanking and disciplining service to women…

Discover an underworld of sex, spanking and submission. A world where high-powered executives and cuddly mums go to be spanked, caned and disciplined.

In this powerful and compelling book Peter reveals how his fetish was kindled by corporal punishment while still at school. How he struggled to contain it until, eventually, he discovered he was far from alone in London's vibrant, active sex scene.

What he learnt on the scene helped him to understand the psychology of women who wanted to submit to submissive discipline. Many were professional women, often juggling a demanding job and family. They needed to occasionally relinquish all control, to submit totally to the will of another. Others sought a father figure who could offer them the firm security they remembered from their childhood when Daddy had been very much in control.

Chapter by chapter he reveals his clients' stories as he turns their fantasies into reality. The writing is powerful, the stories graphic and compelling.

Discover an unknown world…

ISBN 9781906373313   Price £9.99

Also from Xcite Books

Sex & Seduction	**1905170785**	**price £7.99**
Sex & Satisfaction	**1905170777**	**price £7.99**
Sex & Submission	**1905170793**	**price £7.99**
5 Minute Fantasies 1	**1905170610**	**price £7.99**
5 Minute Fantasies 2	**190517070X**	**price £7.99**
5 Minute Fantasies 3	**1905170718**	**price £7.99**
Whip Me	**1905170920**	**price £7.99**
Spank Me	**1905170939**	**price £7.99**
Tie Me Up	**1905170947**	**price £7.99**
Ultimate Sins	**1905170599**	**price £7.99**
Ultimate Sex	**1905170955**	**price £7.99**
Ultimate Submission	**1905170963**	**price £7.99**

www.xcitebooks.com